Also by Karen M. Dillon

The Immortal Souls: Magic & Chaos
Immortal Souls
Guardian Vampire
Demonic Recruit

For more book updates visit:
evilbunnybooks.com

or follow me on:
facebook.com/evilbunnybooks
twitter.com/evilbunnybooks

KAREN M. DILLON

THE
IMMORTAL
SOULS

MAGIC & CHAOS
BOOK THREE

The Evil Bunny, First Edition 2017

ISBN: 978-0-9929481-4-6
eBook ISBN: 978-0-9929481-5-3

Cover and layout design © 2016 Karen M. Dillon

Edited by Josh Brookes

<u>**AUTHOR'S NOTE:**</u>

What you're about to read is the first edition of The Immortal Souls Book 3: Demonic Recruit.

However, for those of you who are not aware, in October & December of 2016, I released a new edition of the first two books in this series—the overall plot remains the same, however there are some newer scenes that have been added into the first two books that may help fill in some of the plot gaps that were in the original editions.

The electronic version of the first two books (if the electronic version was the one you purchased) should be available for free if you already purchased the original edition. You should be able to redownload the newer edition from the site you purchased it from with no extra cost—specific instructions on how to get the updated version vary so you should refer to the site of purchase for specific instructions on how to proceed with getting the updated editions.

Unfortunately if you purchased this book through the hard copy paperback edition, then there is no automatic update (sorry).

However, if you can provide me with proof of purchase of the paperback I would be more than happy to send you a free

PDF copy of the new editions. Message me on Facebook or Twitter for info/details.

Thanks for reading, and I hope you're enjoying the story so far.

HUGS & KISSES FROM

Karen

THE
IMMORTAL
SOULS

DEMONIC RECRUIT

For my Mam,

Who waited 3 books to read her favourite scene
Which used to be Book 1, Chapter 2.

CHAPTER 1

"You're an idiot."

Sam slowly pushed the duvet off her face and looked up at Jack, glaring. Though, by the expression on Jack's face it was clear that he couldn't care less that she was glaring, as he could probably tell her heart wasn't really in it.

"*Thanks,*" she sneered with as much sarcasm as she could muster.

"You're welcome," Jack replied, smiling widely. "You are though . . . An idiot, I mean."

"Whose side are you *on?*"

"There are no sides," he said carefully, giving her a measured glance. "And Jamie was right to say what he said." Sam opened her mouth to speak, but Jack held up a hand to stop her. "He *was.* You know he was. You were being unreasonable, and to be honest it's about time someone, *besides* me, called you on your bullshit."

Sam gave Jack the most hateful expression she could. "So

you think I'm a spoiled child?" she said. "You think I'm a user and a manipulator?" She tried to bite back her tears, but couldn't stop them from escaping. "Are you *done* with me too?"

Jack let a frustrated sigh, rolling his eyes. "Yes, yes, yes and no."

Sam huffed and pulled the duvet over her head. Cocooning herself in the blanket so tightly she would most likely be suffocated. The mattress sank slightly behind her. She expected Jack to be sitting on the side of her bed trying to think of some kind words that would make her feel better, or to think of a way to apologise for causing her even more upset.

But instead, his weight lifted, and before Sam could fully unravel herself from the duvet to see where the hell he was going, Jack's entire weight slammed into her. She screamed a little, the impact surprising her more than it actually hurt. He lay on his side, his body stretched over her as he pushed his entire weight into her.

Then he bounced up and down. "Stop . . . Being . . . Stupid."

"Did you just body slam me!"

Jack stopped moving, looking at her with an expression of complete sincerity. "If I have to wrestle the idiocy out of you, I will. And I'm a trained combatant *and* immune to your Magic, so you *know* I'll win."

"How am I being stupid?" Sam asked, wondering what exactly it was that Jack believed she'd done wrong, and more than that what exactly he expected her to do. As far as she was concerned she'd done nothing wrong.

Jamie was the one who started an argument with her.

He was the one who called her names.

He was the one who should apologise.

Did Jack expect her to behave like some kind of needy

stalker? To go to Jamie's house and to follow him around begging him to come back to her?

The likelihood of that happening was completely non-existent.

It wasn't even as though they'd ever been together in the first place.

He was just some random creeper who'd started hanging around her that she'd never actually gotten around to getting rid of.

The main point of it was that Jamie had upset her, and if he wanted to talk again *he* could apologise. She'd been fine before him, she'd be fine without him.

"I know what you're thinking," Jack said, watching her with an expression that indicated he *did*. "And you're wrong. You need to learn to accept responsibility for the things you do Sam. You're eighteen, it's about time you stopped acting like a precious spoiled baby and learned to grow up."

Sam looked at Jack in disbelief, struggling against his weight while she attempted to push herself into a sitting position.

But Jack didn't move, and as his corporeal form was heavier than she could lift she was forced to give up, and with a sigh she let herself drop back to the mattress. "*I* didn't *do* anything. He called me names, *he* upset *me*."

Jack shook his head disapprovingly. "Let me give you the entire list of things you've done wrong to date."

"What!"

"One, you erased his memories in the library."

Sam rolled her eyes and let a sigh. "Technically that doesn't even count. It didn't work, because for some reason he's immune to me."

Jack gave her a sideways glance. "It's the fact that you tried. Number two, when he *risked his life* to help you, you ran off and let him go on believing you were human."

"Bu—"

"Three, when he came to call you out, you scared him by calling him a Vampire and let him spend a whole day being scared and confused for your own entertainment."

"Oh com—"

"Four, you were so difficult that he had to kidnap you to get you to tell him the truth. *And*, you wouldn't even have a normal conversation, instead, being as difficult as a Sam can be, you displayed your Magic in a way that scared him."

"You weren't even—"

"Five—"

"You can't list *everything!*" Sam yelled over Jack, letting out her frustration at being cut off over and over.

Jack raised an eyebrow and gave her an 'oh, can't I?' expression. "Refused to talk to him. Refused to share your feelings. Accepted his declaration of love, but didn't return it. Led him on. Accused him of being selfish when he did the right thing. Never thanked him for sticking with you when he could have left any time he wanted. Upsetting *him* first and then lying in bed expecting *him* to apologise for *finally* venting. To be honest, I'm surprised it took him so long," Jack added thoughtfully. "With everything you put him through, I expected him to yell at you a lot sooner . . . I would have if I was him."

"So, you're on his side."

"Oh yeah, and changing the subject of conversations instead of being a grown up and facing your own faults."

Sam scowled.

Jack finally sat up, taking his weight off her and giving her room to follow suit. She pushed herself up and sat with her arms folded across her chest.

"Go to his house and apologise."

"I'm not going to go crawling over to him," Sam said, shocked that Jack would even suggest it. "If he wants to see me he can—"

"No," Jack interrupted, looking her right in the eyes and pointing a finger in her direction. "*You* go to his house and *apologise*. It is the very least he deserves from you. You don't need to crawl, you can use a portal, or walk, or run . . . it doesn't matter how you get there, point is, *go*. You started it, so it's up to you."

Sam sighed. "What if I don't want to apologise?"

Jack gave her a half smile. "Well then you'll probably never see him again."

"Fine," she said with a half-hearted shrug. "I don't even care."

"So . . . you've been sitting up here sulking for the past two days because you're *not* upset that he said he never wants to see you again?"

"I'm not sulking," Sam said defensively. Technically it was true. For the past two days she'd been doing a lot more than merely sulking.

With his hand, Jack directed to her face. "So this whole red eye runny mascara look is supposed to be some kind of new fashion trend?"

Sam self-consciously lifted a hand to her face, and felt around her eye for makeup. And sure enough, when she took her hand away, there were black smudges. *Waterproof my ass,* she thought with an internal sigh. "Maybe it is," she mumbled.

Jack placed a hand on her shoulder. The heat of his skin surprising her as it always did.

Something Sam had always wondered about was why his skin was never cold. She always thought of Ghosts being made of ice, but right now Jack's skin was warm, almost hot.

She raised her eyes to meet his.

"Go apologise," he said with a kind smile. "You need him, and he needs you. And I honestly can't stand any more of this whingeing. So apologise before I have to hit you."

Before Sam had a chance to reply, Jack vanished.

She sighed, looking at the empty space where he'd been sitting a moment ago, thinking of how one day he *wouldn't* get to have the last word.

CHAPTER 2

$\mathscr{J}$ack left Sam alone to mope, hoping against the odds that he'd managed to irritate her enough into—at the very least—getting out of bed. With a sigh, he rematerialised in the hallway, looking briefly over his shoulder at Sam's locked door before he turned and made his way towards the attic.

He could hear Danny speaking from the bottom of the staircase, and when he actually entered the room Jack found him on the phone rather than doing the job he'd been assigned.

Locating Sam's amulet and, subsequently, the boy who stole it—their only *real* connection to the U.I.E.

With a scowl directed at the back of Danny's head, Jack made his way over to Jade, who was sitting on one of the wooden chairs that surrounded the table on the far end of the room. She sat staring with unseeing eyes into a black cauldron filled with water.

"Have you two found anything yet?" he asked as he approached.

She sighed and shook her head. "No, there's no sign of anyone . . . well, at least—" she directed to the water, then sighed. "It's not like I could really tell you anyway, I'm not like you guys."

Jack placed a hand on her shoulder. "Magic is easily learned by anyone, Jade, that includes you too."

She shrugged, then turned her attention back to the water, which reflected nothing. "Why isn't he working?" Jack asked, directing to Danny.

Jade briefly looked in Danny's direction. "He's talking to the school, they want to know why Sam's been absent . . . again."

Jack scoffed. "There's more important things to do."

"Yeah, well, he still needs to explain it away or they'll kick her out."

Jack shook his head as he stared towards the window, watching the back garden through a gap in the curtains. He really did wish that Sam would stop wasting her time attempting to be human. If she hadn't been raised in this society perhaps she'd be less of a whiner and more of a doer.

Maybe she would actually do the things that needed to be done instead of wasting her time playing pretend.

CHAPTER 3

Sam had spent maybe twenty minutes alone in her room, thinking about what Jack said to her. After a few minutes of repeating his words again and again inside her head, she realised that he may have had a point. And so, slowly and reluctantly, she got herself out of bed, showered, made herself look like she *hadn't* been in bed for two days, and took a portal to Jamie's house.

The portal left her less than a five minute walk from it.

It was the middle of the day and since Jamie was no longer accompanying her to school—not that she'd actually gone— she figured the odds were he'd still be asleep. For a moment, she stood by the trees where she'd carved runes of protection and misdirection, and hesitated. Thinking maybe she should go away and come back later, or perhaps call first. She wasn't the best with words, especially not when she was face to face with other people. Perhaps it would be easier over the phone . . . or by email.

She took a breath and decided to keep moving forward. If she left and went home she knew she would be less likely to do anything at all.

When she was at the door she stopped for a moment, wondering exactly what she should say.

Would sorry be enough, or would he expect some kind of speech?

She closed her hand up tightly, and with her fist banged on the door.

It was about five seconds later that the door opened and Jamie stood there, fully dressed in jeans and a long sleeved sweater, giving the impression he'd been awake for hours even though his hair was tousled and his feet were bare. He looked at her with wide eyes, as though he was surprised to see her standing outside his house, but then slowly his expression turned to one of stone. "What do you want?" he asked, folding his arms across his chest.

"I wanted to talk to you," Sam said, placing both hands behind her back as she stood there.

Jamie let a sigh. "Now's not a good time," he said. "I'm busy."

Sam raised an eyebrow. "Busy?" she asked, wondering what he could possibly be doing. He didn't really *do* anything, so how could he be busy?

He nodded, his expression impatient. "Yeah," he said. *"Busy."*

"Are you just saying that because you don't want to talk to me?"

He smiled humourlessly and looked down at the ground. "Still think everything is about you I see."

Sam let a sigh, feeling annoyed and unsure as to whether she was annoyed at him or herself. "Look . . . I ca—"

"Jamie?"

Sam stopped speaking, surprised to hear the sound of someone else. And even more surprised to hear that the voice was female. She searched Jamie's face for some kind of explanation, feeling more hurt than she thought she would to find that he had a girl in his house.

He looked over his shoulder at whoever it was that had spoken.

"Who is it?" the woman asked.

Jamie slowly turned his gaze to Sam; his expression seemed pleading and his eyes looked tired. He let an irritated sigh as a woman with long brown hair pulled on the door and stood beside him. She looked at Sam curiously. The feeling of hurt quickly turned to one of anger when she noticed that the woman was pretty and not only that but she was wearing men's pyjamas, which Sam could only assume did not belong to her.

After a moment of wondering why she was careful not to step too far outside the shade of the house, Sam noticed the aura that surrounded her and realised she was a Vampire. For a minute she thought that maybe this woman had been sent here by Aleczander to check up on Jamie.

That seemed like something Aleczander might have done.

"Oh," the woman said, blinking in surprise when she saw Sam.

After a moment, Jamie sighed and said, "Sam, this is —"

"Bethany." The woman extended her hand. Sam reached out, about to take it, when Bethany continued. "Jamie's wife."

Sam froze, letting her hand fall back to her side; she stared at Jamie, dumbfounded, while he stared at Bethany, clearly shocked that she'd chosen to introduce herself like that. "Bethany," he said, his tone filled with impatience. "Can you *please* give me a minute?"

She looked at Jamie for a moment, as if she were confused

at why she wasn't wanted for this conversation, then slowly nodded her head. After she'd walked back inside, Jamie stepped out and closed the door behind him.

"Sam—" he started, but Sam cut him off.

"You have a *wife*?"

He sighed and ran his hand through his hair. "It's really not as simple as that."

"Oh?" she said, glaring at him for a moment. She let an irate grumble. "Tell me this *just* happened. That over the past two days you got *really* drunk and it *just* happened."

Jamie paused for a moment, chewing his lip as he looked at her with a guilty expression on his face. "Are you fucking serious?" Sam yelled. "So, what? Was she on vacation for the past four months or something?"

"No!" Jamie said, gazing at Sam as if willing her to understand.

"So then you just didn't have her here when I was here?"

He shook his head. "No," he said again. "Would you just—"

"And you called *me* a user? You're a fucking liar!" Sam snapped. She tightened her hand into a fist and seriously contemplated the possibility of beating the shit out of him.

"That's not fair," he said, his mouth set in a harsh line as he glared at her. "You have *no* idea wha—"

"Shut up!" Sam interrupted. "I don't want to talk to you!"

She turned and walked away from him, half expecting him to reach out to stop her, or to follow in her step. But instead he just yelled at her from where he stood. "If you don't want to talk to me, then don't come to my house!"

Sam clenched her jaw in anger as she stormed off, hearing a door slam behind her.

She didn't look back.

Just kept on walking towards the portal that would take her

home.

CHAPTER 4

*J*amie stood with his back pressed to the inside of the door, breathing hard through his anger. He closed his eyes for a moment, half wondering why Sam had come to see him. It must have been something of importance if she was willing to show her face here. He knew Sam, and after the argument they'd had the last time they'd spoken he'd walked away knowing there was no chance of her speaking to him again.

Yet there she was.

As soon as he'd seen her face there had been a moment in which he'd forgotten how furious he was with her, a moment when his breath caught in his throat and his stomach flipped.

A moment when he felt elated at the sight of her.

But then he'd remembered.

And once again he'd ended their argument by, more or less, telling her that he never wanted to see her again.

He opened his eyes when he felt Bethany's proximity, she

froze when he'd opened his eyes and she looked at him curiously. Curiosity was an expression she seemed to wear quite frequently.

She was watching him as if she were looking at someone she knew yet didn't recognise. For a moment, Jamie wondered if he had really changed that much. It wasn't something he had ever really considered. Each day he looked in the mirror he appeared exactly the same as he had the day before, so an ability to change was not something he'd ever considered possible.

Not until he saw Bethany look at him with that expression *again*.

"Is everything alright?" she asked.

Jamie nodded his head, pushing himself away from the door.

"That girl," Bethany said. "Is she . . . is she your girlfriend?"

Jamie shook his head. "No, she's not my girlfriend."

"*Was* she?"

Again, Jamie shook his head.

The relationship between he and Sam was a complicated one to explain and he didn't feel like trying now, but the one thing he knew for certain was that Sam wasn't, nor had she ever been, his girlfriend.

Bethany smiled. "What did she want?"

Jamie shrugged. "She didn't say."

"But—"

"If you don't mind," Jamie snapped irately, "I'd rather not talk about it."

Giving him the same confused expression, Bethany nodded. Jamie rubbed his eyes with the back of his hands, he'd been awake since Bethany had arrived on his doorstep in the early hours of the morning. Through the day he'd let her sleep in his bed, while he stayed downstairs, extremely confused as to how it was possible for her to be here.

"I didn't expect you to be awake just yet," he said. The sun wouldn't set for another few hours, and from what he remembered of her Bethany never awoke until after sunset.

She smiled. "I heard a knock at the door and was curious."

Jamie nodded his head, sitting himself down on the sofa. "You could go back to sleep if you wanted."

Bethany sat down beside him, closer than he necessarily wanted. "Did you sleep down here?" she asked, looking around the living room.

"No," he said. "I've been awake."

"Are you tired?"

He shook his head despite the fact that he was exhausted. "I'll sleep later tonight."

"Tonight?" she asked, giving him a curious glance. "I was wondering . . . how you went outside and didn't get hurt. Did something . . . *how* did that happen?"

Jamie opened his mouth to answer, and for a moment considered telling her about the amulet Sam had given him. But he hesitated for long enough that he noticed a feeling of apprehension forming in the pit of his stomach, and somehow he just knew it would be a bad idea to tell her the truth. Trying hard not to look at the ring he wore for fear of drawing attention to it, he shrugged and forced a smile. "It's not important," he said, taking a page out of Sam's 'how to avoid unwanted conversation' book. "Anyway, tell me what happened."

Bethany pulled at a loose thread at the end of the t-shirt he'd given her to sleep in. "Is *that* important?"

Jamie sighed. "Bethany . . . You said that you thought *I* was dead. And I don't understand how because *you* died. Not me."

"But—"

"I *saw* you," he said, turning to face her. "I was there. I saw you killed. I buried you. I mourned you. It's been—" he sighed. "It's been a *long* time. And you show up on my doorstep, saying that you've been alive all along. So *yes*, I believe an explanation is important. How am I to know you're you? How do I know you're not someone else? Some*thing* else?"

She laughed slightly. "Who else would I be?" she asked. "What else is there to be?"

Jamie looked at her, his expression serious. "You'd be surprised at the amount of other things there are to be. And how many of them have the ability to wear someone else's face."

CHAPTER 5

$\mathcal{S}$am groaned when she felt Jack sit down on the side of her bed. "Go! Away!"

She heard Jack sigh as the duvet was pulled from her face, leaving her lying on her bed completely exposed to the cold air and daylight that filled her room. "Did I *not* say I was sick of your whingeing?"

Sam pushed herself into a sitting position and glared at Jack. "I think I have *every* right to be pissed off with him."

"So what you're saying is you *didn't* apologise."

"No," Sam said. "I didn't apologise, I was too distracted by his *wife* being present."

Sam felt a brief moment of satisfaction when she saw Jack's eyes go wide with shock as his brain processed what he'd just heard. "His what now?"

"Yeah," Sam said. "His wife. He's married and apparently while I was busy not sharing personal things, he was *hiding* personal things. Being married is kind of the first thing you tell someone, right?"

Jack nodded his head, then his expression turned thoughtful. "Did he say she was his wife?"

"Oh no," Sam said. "*She* did. She said, 'Hi, I'm Jamie's wife.'"

"And what did he say?"

Sam shrugged, folding her arms across her chest. It didn't matter what he said, or what he had to say. The entire situation said enough for itself.

Jack gave her a sideways glance. "Did you give him a chance to speak before you freaked out?"

Sam gaped at him. "Are you *seriously* trying to tell me I'm in the wrong?"

Jack shrugged. "He's been around for a *long* time, back in his day people got married young. Maybe he was married before he was Turned, maybe he got married after. Either way, if he's been here for what, quarter of a century, and the Coven say he's the *only* Vampire living here, the odds are they've been separated for years. He could be just as surprised to see her as you were. My point *is* did you ask him, or give him a chance to say?"

"I shouldn't have to!" Sam yelled. "I shouldn't have to have that conversation at all!"

Jack sighed, chewing his lip for a moment before he asked, "What year was he born?"

Sam looked at him curiously for a moment, unsure as to why he was asking. "What?"

"What year was he born?"

Sam shrugged, and Jack smiled, which meant she was proving his point though she had no idea what it was. "What year was he Turned?"

Again, Sam shrugged.

"What were his parent's names? Did he have siblings?

Where is he from? What has he been doing for the past two centuries?"

Sam could only stare at him blankly.

"Do you even know what his favourite film is?"

Sam shrugged, unsure as to why any of those things were important.

"So what you're saying is you know *nothing* about him . . . and you're now angry that he didn't tell you the big personal things, when you didn't even want to know the tiniest thing about him?"

"Well, yeah," Sam said. "It's the sort of thing you mention."

"Have you ever *asked* him anything about himself?" Jack asked. "Did you ever show *any* interest?"

Sam opened her mouth to answer, but Jack cut her off. "He hurt your feelings and he should apologise to you for it, *but* you have a lot of things to be sorry for too. So stop feeling sorry for yourself and be the bigger man."

Sam let an irate sigh as Jack vanished suddenly.

"Stop leaving before I can tell you you're wrong!" Sam yelled to the empty room.

CHAPTER 6

ethany sat and chewed her lip as Jamie watched her patiently despite the fact that he had little patience left.

The longer the silence stretched between them the darker his thoughts grew. The more his anger seemed to direct itself towards Bethany, like a cancerous hatred growing in the depths of his body that made him feel an immense urge to physically hurt her for everything she'd put him through.

Making him miss her when she didn't need to be missed.

Making him wait this long when he'd asked her a perfectly reasonable question.

Making Sam hate him by even being here at all.

The thought scratched at the very edge of his mind that if he hurt her — took out his anger on her — he'd feel better about all of those things.

He'd forget the pain she'd put him through in the past.

The mess she was making of his life in the present.

The way she made Sam look at him, as though he'd been the one to do something wrong, when Sam was the one who kept insisting there was nothing between them in the first place.

Unable to dwell on thoughts of him and Sam lest his head explode from the pressure, he sighed and shook his head causing the thoughts to dissipate.

Bethany let a long, heavy breath, twirling the ends of her long chestnut coloured hair between her fingers. He could tell by the expression she wore that she was trying quite hard to think of her answer, and briefly he wondered if he should even believe anything she said. Surely, if it was taking so long to speak, she must have been attempting to get her story straight.

Jamie looked at her with scepticism, for the first time wondering what her motives for tracking him down were.

"Why are you looking at me like that?" she asked, her eyes wide and seeming slightly concerned.

Usually, Jamie would have smiled to comfort her, but there was a feeling stirring inside him that held his features frozen in an expression of severity. "The longer you take to answer me, the more I think you're probably concocting a lie to tell me." He stood and stared down at her, knowing that the sudden difference in their height made him seem imposing. "And then I think that I should change my question from how are you alive, to what are you doing here?"

She answered quickly. "I came to see you."

"Why?" he asked. "Why come to see me now? You've spent almost two centuries away from me, so wh—"

She stood quickly, and before Jamie realised what was happening, she had her lips pressed to his. Too stunned to move, he simply stood there, his body rigid as she stood on her toes and leaned in closer, wrapping her arms around his shoulders as she kissed him.

When he'd first seen her outside his house, memories of their time together had flooded through his mind, filling his chest with a feeling of happiness the same feeling he'd had when they'd first begun their relationship.

But it hadn't been long after, perhaps just a few seconds, that those memories abandoned his thoughts and left him with a hollow feeling, the same thing he'd felt for the first time shortly after he'd lost her.

Even now, with their lips pressed together and not an inch of space between them, he still felt hollow. And he realised that he was not feeling sorrow over the time he'd lost with Bethany, but sorrow over the loss of Sam.

It was then that he pushed her away.

He held her away from him as she stared, her head tilted to the side in bewilderment, her expression seeming slightly hurt. "Don't do that," he said, shaking his head. "I don't want you to do that."

"But wh—"

"Just," he held up a hand to silence her, "go back to sleep."

"What?"

With an irritated sigh he placed a hand on her forehead, sending out a blast of Power which caused her to fall into unconsciousness. He lay her down on the sofa, taking a moment to assess her. She looked just as he remembered, and she treated him as though they'd never been apart.

He didn't like that.

As far as he was concerned you couldn't stay away from someone for that amount of time and then just walk back into their lives as if nothing had ever happened.

With a sigh he turned and walked out the front door. Unsure as to where he would go, but knowing it would be somewhere far from here.

CHAPTER 7

*I*t was about half ten, and Jamie had spent most of the day wandering aimlessly before he ended up at Sam's house.

He'd been on the roof alone for the better part of an hour before Jack appeared out of nowhere and sat himself beside Jamie. "Do you just hang out here?"

Jamie shrugged, looking out at the darkened street with a calm disinterest. "I used to sit on my own roof to think, but—"

"You can't now that your wife is home?"

Jamie felt himself flinch at the word wife. It had been so long since he'd considered himself to have one, and hearing people say it felt wrong. "She's not really, you know," he said. "I loved her once a *long* time ago. I thought she was dead, I mourned her, I moved on. And she expects that everything will be the same as it was. But as far as I'm concerned, she's not my wife."

"Okay . . . So here you are, on Sam's roof, a wifeless man — "

"I'm not here to see Sam," he stated. "I just needed somewhere to sulk."

"So it's true then?"

Jamie turned to Jack and looked at him curiously, wondering what it was he was talking about. "Sam told me you said you were done with her."

Jamie nodded his head. "I did say that."

"And you meant it?"

He let a tired sigh. "I'm done going along with her manipulations, I will *not* be used for her amusement."

"She loves you, you know?" Jamie gave him a sceptical glance, confused as to how he had managed to come to that conclusion. Unless Sam had told Jack something she hadn't said to him? It was possible, considering the fact that she seemed to trust Jack more than anyone else, making Jack basically the only person Sam would be likely to confide in.

Although, somehow, he highly doubted that Sam had ever confessed to having any feelings of love, for Jamie or for anyone.

"She does," Jack insisted.

"How would *you* know?"

"You didn't know her before," Jack said, gazing out at the empty street. "After everything that happened, she got really depressed, she stopped going out, stopped having fun, stopped making an effort. She would always wear these hideous, loose fitting, baggy comfort clothes, never did her hair up nice or made herself look pretty or anything. She kinda just stopped . . . *everything*. Because of that, I knew she loved you the day after you met."

Jamie raised an eyebrow and looked at Jack quizzically. "It's true," he said with a smile. "I knew it because when I came back she was wearing a skirt. I didn't even know she owned skirts anymore. She had make-up on, her hair was down and nice and she was wearing perfume."

Jamie couldn't help smiling at the idea of Sam dressing up, making herself smell nice, for *him*. "She was?"

Jack nodded. "I won't lie, even dressed in frumpy clothes Sam looks gorgeous and a *lot* of boys, and men, and girls, and women, pay attention to her. But she never gave any of them a second glance . . . or even a first glance until the day she saw you. And she was smiling, happier than I'd ever seen her, and the moment you saw her use her Magic and she erased your memories and she thought she'd never see you again, she sulked more epically than you are right now."

"I need to hear her say it," Jamie said with a sigh. "I was going off the assumption that she cared about me but didn't want to say it. But I can't do that anymore. Just because I'm immortal doesn't mean I'll wait around forever. I need her to tell me, but she won't. So how can I possibly believe she does?"

"Some things are worth waiting forever for."

"I've travelled the world," Jamie said. "That's what I spent the past two centuries doing, travelling. I've been to every country, seen all the sites. I have a basement full of collectables and souvenirs. I never planned to stay here, you know . . . This was just a place I was passing through about twenty-something years ago."

"So why did you stay?"

Jamie shrugged. "Something about this place . . . I felt like there was something important, so I settled. But then I met Sam and I realised that maybe I was waiting for her. And maybe I feel like I've been waiting for long enough."

"Love isn't something that just happens," Jack said. "It's the sort of thing that creeps up on you, the sort of thing you spend months denying, a feeling you assess before you realise that it's true. When you were starting out in the world, you were in a time when proclamations of love were made quickly, you could make eye contact with someone and that would be enough. Sam is from now, where it takes more than just seeing someone to love them. It will take time for her to get there.

"It's been, what? Three . . . four months since you met her?"

Jamie nodded his head.

"That's four months of a lifetime, an *immortal* lifetime, which is *nothing*. If you love her like you claim to, you'll wait for as long as it takes."

"So now, you're saying that I don't love her?"

Jack shrugged. "Young people confuse infatuation and love so easily. Love is hard but it lasts, infatuation is easy and it fades. If you can really be done with her so easily, it's because you didn't love her like you thought you did."

Jamie was about to protest, but Jack was gone before he got the chance.

He listened out, expecting to hear the sound of Jack's voice from inside the house, but he didn't. The only sound from inside was the TV in the living room. Jamie sighed, slightly disappointed. He kind of imagined that Jack would act as his go between, thinking that anything he said about Sam to Jack would be passed along.

He listened closer and heard that there were three heartbeats in the house. Two downstairs, the other upstairs.

Slowly, Jamie climbed down from the roof, hanging onto the rain gutters. He shimmied along a little before he dropped, grabbing onto the windowsill outside Sam's bedroom. Peering through the gap in the curtains he could see Sam sitting curled up on her bed, wearing a t-shirt and nothing more.

He froze for a moment.

He'd never given much, or any thought, to Sam's sleeping attire, but he'd expected her to be wearing more than she was.

Nevertheless, she looked beautiful, sitting in the dim lamplight, in her t-shirt with her hair brushed over one shoulder, her legs tucked under herself, chewing her lip as she read the book she held in her hands.

Jamie took a breath, and pushed the window open. Briefly noticing her look in his direction as he pulled himself up and perched in the open window. "Is it okay if I come in?" he asked.

She looked at him for a moment, seeming slightly surprised to see him. "What are you doing here?" she asked, both her expression and her tone making it appear as though she didn't want him anywhere near her.

"I would like to talk to you."

She paused before she nodded. Jamie stepped inside, closing the window behind him. He walked over to the bed where she sat—watching him—and seated himself on the edge. "I'm sorry," he said as he let a sigh. "I was a bit harsh the other day . . . and earlier."

"It's okay," she said, placing her book upside down on the mattress. "I think we both know you didn't really do anything wrong. I was being a bitch."

"No—" Jamie tried to protest, but she held up her hand to cut him off.

"I was," she said. "I know I was. I was just upset and I took it out on you, and I shouldn't have."

"Wow . . . " Jamie said, unable to help his surprise. He'd expected Sam to argue with him, or to just accept his apology and then go back to behaving as she had before.

"I know," she said, with a smile. "Jack already yelled at me. It's why I went to see you, I was going to apologise, then I found out you had a *wife*, and may have forgotten why I went in the first place . . . then Jack yelled at me again."

"He yelled at you for being upset?"

Sam shook her head. "He yelled at me for being an idiot. He does that a lot. Basically, what he said was I need to stop blaming everyone for things I do wrong and I need to learn to take responsibility, and then he said you were right to call me a spoiled child because I am. I tried to protest, his argument was better." She shook her head. "He should be a professional arguer, if that's even a thing."

Jamie smiled. "I think the closest thing would be a lawyer."

Sam leaned forward, and before he had a moment to process what was happening, she had her arms wrapped around his neck and her chin resting on his shoulder. "I'm sorry," she said.

Jamie wrapped his arms around her waist, and slowly pulled her forward so she was resting on his lap. "Did it physically hurt you to say that?" he asked, a small grin curving his lips.

She winced slightly. "I was in less pain that time Jack punched me in the face," she said, repositioning her head so that her cheek rested on his shoulder.

He laughed. "I'll have take a mental picture so I can frame this moment and add it to my basement collection of memories. I'll call it *the first – and possibly only – time Sam ever apologised.*"

"Basement?" Sam pushed her head away from him so she could stare at him in confusion. "Your house doesn't have a basement."

Jamie smiled. "It does," he said. "There's a secret door in the living room, underneath the rug."

"You mean to say that you have a secret door and I never knew about it?"

Jamie laughed.

"What else are you hiding in there?"

"Quite a bit," he admitted. "I've collected a lot of things over the past few years, and there's no room in the house for them."

"Things like?"

Jamie shrugged. "I can show you if you want."

"Maybe some other time," Sam said with a sigh. "In case you haven't noticed I'm already in my jammies."

"I *did* notice," he said with a smile, his eyes drifting down to the bare skin of her legs. "You look very nice by the way."

"I like to be cosy," Sam said, casually fiddling with the end of her t-shirt. "Magic keeps me warm so there's no need for pants." With a devious smile she added, "Occasionally there's no need for a shirt either."

Jamie almost choked as he gawped at her. "What?"

An amused smile spread across her face and she began to laugh. "Sometimes," she said through her laughter, "it's just too easy to mess with you."

"That was a cruel joke," he said, though he was smiling, his eyes half shut as he gazed down at her sitting on his lap in a piece of clothing that was so thin it may as well not have been there at all, and imagining — without much effort — that it *wasn't.* "You shouldn't toy with my emotions like that."

He looked up, redirecting his attention to Sam's eyes, and when he did he found her to be watching him with a strange expression on her face. For a moment, he stared back, wondering why she watched him as she did. It was only when he'd focused his senses away from his own thoughts that he heard it.

The hard thrumming of her heart.

He gazed at her expectantly, waiting for her to kiss him as she had so brazenly in times before. But she didn't, and the lack of action disappointed him more than it probably should have. After all, he had been the one to ask her not to behave like that towards him, and here she was, kindly obliging to his request, though it was obvious by her speeding pulse and the way she looked at him that she didn't want to. It was then that he realised the strange expression in her eyes had been the same expression he now looked to her with, expectation. She had agreed not to kiss him, but he hadn't made any such agreements.

Before Jamie had time to fully think the situation through, he leaned forward, filling the small space that separated them, and pressed his lips to hers, meaning for the kiss to be a delicate one, a sign of how he loved her. But when he pressed his lips to hers, breathing in her breath, and feeling her move her body closer, he lost all sense of inhibition. Wrapping his arms around her and holding onto her tightly, he kissed her fervently as he was overcome by a lustful sensation.

She responded without hesitation, returning his passion with equal enthusiasm, running her hands through his hair as she attempted to move herself even closer.

But the position they were currently in — with her sitting on his lap — had her twisted at an awkward angle, making it difficult for their bodies to press close enough together.

So — not releasing her from his arms — he turned so that they were lying on her bed.

Sam placed her arms around his neck and pulled him closer, wrapping her legs around him as she did. He placed a hand on her leg, slowly moving it upwards, along the smooth skin of her thigh, lifting up the end of her t-shirt as his hand moved upwards, pausing momentarily as his fingers touched off the elastic hem of her underwear. Moving slowly, taking the time to savour the sensation of touching her skin, resisting the urge to tear the fabric from her body as he desired to, he moved past, his hand reaching the curve of her hip.

Then Sam seemed to lose her patience, and with a sigh she turned, flipping him over so that she was straddling him as he lay on his back. She leaned in and kissed him, harder and faster than before. Their kisses becoming more fervent and desperate as they clung to each other.

Grabbing onto the collar of his jacket, she pulled him up so that he was sitting with her still on top of him. Without wasting a second, she tore the jacket from his body and threw it to the floor. Jamie pulled her closer, his fingers entangled in her hair as her hands moved down his body towards his belt.

The door opened suddenly and Sam's body froze, her head snapping in the direction of the intruder. With an irate sigh, Jamie glared at Jade, briefly thinking that if he killed her now he and Sam could continue uninterrupted.

The casualness of this violent thought gave him pause, and with a feeling of sudden clarity he realised what he was doing and he quickly let Sam go, moving himself away from her.

"Nice," Jade said, apparently unfazed by the scene she'd walked in on. "I'm ordering Chinese food, either of you want any?"

"Uh . . . " Sam shook her head. "No, I'm okay."

Jade shrugged, and began to back out of the doorway, pausing before she closed it to smile at them. "It's good that we're all friends again, but you guys should probably do that somewhere else. If Danny walks in—" she paused for a moment, seeming to think. "—Call me, the fight that breaks out would get a billion views on YouTube, and I want to be the one to upload it."

With that, the door slammed shut. And Jamie felt a sudden wash of shame break over him at how he had behaved. He stood, and walked to the corner of Sam's room, staring down at the carpet as he attempted to figure out the cause of his outburst, taking a few deep breaths to calm himself.

"What's wrong?" Sam asked, her voice sounding concerned.

"I'm sorry," he said, placing a hand to his head as he shook it. "I shouldn't have done that."

"Why not?"

Jamie peered at her over his shoulder. She sat on the edge of her bed, seeming confused.

"Because, you don't—" He stopped himself, his mind going back to the words Jack had spoken earlier.

Time.

Sam needed time and he realised that it was wrong of him to try push her. She would share her feelings when she felt it was right for her. He sighed and turned around to face her. "I just shouldn't have attacked you like that, it was inappropriate."

For a moment Sam simply watched him, as though she was assessing him, and then she smiled slightly. "I suppose I'll forgive you just this one time." She seemed sarcastic in her words and, despite the fact that Jamie had been sincere in his apology, he smiled.

"I guess we'll have to have conversation then," Sam sighed and rolled her eyes. "You may have noticed that I have a hard time speaking about things. Anything that involves feelings and anything about *before*. But, I guess that's not really fair, so I'll participate in a conversation, just tonight . . . and then we can all move on with our lives."

Jamie paused, wondering where this decision had suddenly come from, then he remembered how she'd said Jack had yelled at her, and realised that he must have mentioned something about her communication issues. He considered her proposition for a moment, finding the idea of being able to ask Sam anything alluring, but then he smiled and shook his head. "No."

Sam looked him directly in the eyes, her expression one of complete incomprehension. "No?"

"No. There will be no conversational participation for you." She raised an eyebrow and looked at him quizzically. "It wouldn't be fair for me to ask you about things that I know you're uncomfortable talking about. So, here's how our conversations will work. You can ask me personal questions all you like and I'll answer. Because that's what I do. And I'll ask you a variety of things that may or may not have anything to do with anything. And you'll either answer them, or not. Because that's what you do. And then one day . . . maybe five million years from now, you'll tell me something personal. Like your favourite flavour of ice-cream."

Sam grinned widely. "Jack yelled at you too, didn't he?"

"It doesn't matter how much sense you make . . . he always manages to win."

Sam looked thoughtful for a moment. "I suppose I should have asked stuff before, then I would have . . . well, probably not. I mean the odds of me asking if you had a wife were never very high."

"Because you wouldn't have cared, or —"

Sam wrapped her hand around the wrist of his left hand, then shook it slowly. "Usually, there's no need to ask."

Jamie looked at his hand where his wedding band used to sit. "It's in the basement," he said. "With most of the things I no longer have any need for."

With a small sigh Sam pushed herself back so that she was sitting at the head of the bed, her back pressed against a pile of pillows.

Jamie looked at her for a moment, before he kicked his shoes off his feet, then slid back, seating himself beside her. "So," he said, resting his head awkwardly on the decorative bars that made up the headboard. "Ask me anything."

Sam glanced around thoughtfully, as if trying to come up with a question. "Okay," she said. "I guess . . . start from the start."

Jamie raised an eyebrow as he looked at her. "Life story?"

She shrugged as she picked the book up off the bed and set it down on the table next to the lamp. "Why not?" she asked rhetorically. "I wasn't really into that book anyway. So make this story more interesting."

"Okay," Jamie said with a smile. "Once upon a time I was a baby."

She gave him a sideways glance. "Be serious."

He smiled widely, amused by the expression on her face. "I've been told I was a very endearing baby."

Sam rolled her eyes. "Okay, so once upon a time you were endearing . . . What happened? Where did it all go wrong?"

He let a sigh and tried not to be offended. "I was born in eighteen-oh-one," he spoke quickly and turned to Sam, expecting her to have a smart remark in response to his statement.

But she just watched him for a moment, then said, "What? Why are you staring at me?"

"I was waiting for you to say something about *ye olde ancient times,* as you call it."

Sam smiled and shrugged. "At this point I think that kind of goes without saying."

Jamie sighed. "Should I just start the story right before I was Turned?"

Sam shrugged. "Depends, how interesting was your life before?"

"It was late August, and outside a storm was brewing."

"That's good," Sam said. "Set the scene. August, storm . . . what were you wearing? Just *how* puffy was your shirt?"

Jamie tried not to laugh. "I didn't have a puffy shirt, that was the *seventeen* hundreds."

"Okay, so August, storm, regular shirt. Did you have a ridiculous hairstyle?"

Jamie laughed slightly. "What is your obsession?"

Sam shrugged. "I want to know how stupid you looked so I can be amused and laugh."

With a sigh, he rolled his eyes. "*Anyway* . . . I was at home, packing up my belongings for my trip in the morning."

"Trip?" Sam asked. "Where were you going?"

"Cambridge," he said, folding his arms across his chest. "University. Do you just ignore half of the conversations we have?"

"You said you *almost* went . . . Which means you didn't . . . Which means you really shouldn't talk about it as much as you do."

"*Anyway* . . . I was packing up my belongings, when there was a knock on the door. Usually I wouldn't bother to see who was there, but because of the time and the weather I was curious, so I went down to check."

"Who was it?" Sam asked excitedly. "Was it a demon? Like from another dimension? I've always wanted to open the door to a demon from another dimension . . . *Real* demons . . . not Underworld Demons. Like grotesque monster-dragon-insect-bats."

"Monster-dragon-insect-bats? *Why* would you want that?"

For a moment she simply stared as if the answer to his question was obvious. "Because Underworld Demons are boring."

Jamie stared at her for a moment, his eyes squinted in confusion. "But . . . I mean," he sighed, "why would a demon knock on a door?"

Sam laughed slightly. "Don't be an idiot Jamie, they're from another dimension. *Of course* they'd knock on the door, I mean, it's not like they have doorbells in demon dimensions."

Jamie sighed. "Are you sure you want to hear this? Because you keep interrupting me, and that kind of makes it appear as though you're bored of my story."

Sam shook her head and smiled. "I'm just messing with you. Start again," she said. "I won't say anything, promise."

"Alright . . ." With a sigh, he started again.

CHAPTER 8

$\mathcal{I}$t was late August. Outside the rain pummelled down on the rooftop, cascading down the front of the house in waves. The wind crashed so loudly against the windows that I feared they might smash under the pressure. When storms happen, people always try to attribute meaning to them, like saying they were an omen of events to come or the weather was imitating the mood of the humans on the earth below. But this wasn't that kind of storm, it was simply bad weather.

At least that's all I thought of it at the time.

It was quite late. The sun had set hours beforehand and the moon was completely blocked out by the storm clouds; the sky provided no lighting, so I had extra candles in my room. Usually I wouldn't have bothered, on any other night I probably would have abandoned my plans and gone straight to bed due to the cold. But I had packing to do, so an early slumber wasn't an option.

My mother had told me to have the maids pack my luggage

for me, and when I refused she had offered to do it herself. But I refused again, being too stubborn and particular about what I wanted to have with me. So there I was, packing a suitcase by candlelight, while a storm raged outside.

It was only moments after I finished sorting through my journals and notes and moved on to my clothes that there was a knock on the front door. My immediate thought was that it was the carriage to take me away, but then I laughed at myself when I realised the time and remembered that I wasn't to leave until morning.

Once that realisation had struck I became confused, as I wondered who it was who would be knocking on the door at this hour of night. And as well as that, who would be outside in this kind of weather? I looked towards my half packed suitcase, knowing that I shouldn't walk away from it before the task was complete, then towards the door where outside I knew was the answer to the question that floated through my mind.

I placed the shirt I held in my hand into the suitcase, then I made my way to the door. Pausing once it was opened to peer down the hall.

There was no one there and I could hear no sounds coming from downstairs. So curiously, I left the safety of my bedroom and made my way down the hall to the staircase. At the top of the stairs I crouched down, peering through the banister so I could spy without being seen. I felt my body freeze with shock when I found the entrance to be empty and the front door open, the carpet soaked by the rain.

I stood, unsure as to what had happened.

Slowly, I made my way down the stairs. Only when I got to the bottom did I notice that the wet patches on the carpet were the wrong shade to be rainwater. I felt my throat get tight and my pulse race as my mind frantically thought through all of the possibilities for what could have been spilled on the floor.

Mud.

There were no footprints.

Tea.

There were no broken cups.

Wine.

There was no broken glass.

My mind raced in an attempt to provide me with a pacifying answer, an action which only increased my panic, because I already knew what substance stained the floor.

Blood.

I turned to look over my shoulder, where there were several doors, one of which led to the dining room, another led to a parlour, and another to my father's study. I passed the first two and went straight for my father's study, where I thought I could find him. I attempted to move quickly and lightly, trying not to make a sound in case there was a murderous intruder.

I pushed the door open.

Inside the fire was roaring and my father sat facing it. I could see the top of the newspaper he held in his hand leaning over the arm of his chair. I let a sigh of relief at the sight of him, the fear washing out of my body as I realised that I was not alone in the house. I felt that if my father was there, then we would be safe.

I stepped inside the room with some hesitation, not wanting to disturb him despite the dire circumstances.

"Father," I called.

There was no response.

He's sleeping, my brain told me and I repeated the thought again and again in my mind as I stepped closer to his chair.

He's sleeping.

I reached forward.

He's sleeping.

I placed my hand on his shoulder.

He's sleeping.

I shook him lightly.

He's sleeping.

He didn't move.

I felt the sticky substance on my hand before I saw it, and as I laid my eyes upon my crimson stained fingers a scream escaped from my mouth. As the sound hit my ears I placed my blood free hand over my mouth to stifle the noise, my head turning quickly in the direction of the door I had come through.

I expected to see an imposing man, carrying a large weapon, but out in the hallway there was nothing. No movements and no sounds.

I took a breath to calm myself, pressing my lips together tightly as I held my shaking hands before me. Although I did not want to lay my eyes upon my father for I knew him to be dead, the logical part of my brain demanded visual proof. So with great hesitation I looked at my father's face, biting down hard on my tongue as I saw that his eyes were open and his throat was torn apart. His white shirt soaked with the same blood that stained my hands.

In that moment I felt as though I wanted to lie down beside him and break down in tears, but I didn't. My mind thought of my mother and how I needed to find her before whoever had killed my father did.

So, with none of the bravery I feigned to have, I walked out of the study and to the parlour. Opening the door quickly and looking inside. My insides knotted with fear at what I might find. Thankfully, the room was empty, so I proceeded to check all of the downstairs rooms, finding all of them to be devoid of life.

After I had checked the parlour, the dining room, the kitchen, and even the maid's quarters I turned my attention towards the kitchen window, which I found to be open. It was odd that the window should be open when a storm raged outside; logically they all should have been tightly sealed. Unless of course it was open due to someone sneaking through.

I stepped towards the window with trepidation. It wasn't too high from the ground outside, so anyone would have been able to climb through it without difficulty. However, the gap was narrow. So narrow, that surely no one bigger than a child would have been able to get through it.

I walked out of the kitchen and towards the front door, my brain attempting to piece together what seemed like an impossible puzzle.

That was when I saw her.

Standing in the entrance, where the carpet was stained with blood, was a girl.

A girl, who couldn't have been older than fourteen years of age, stood in a dress made of scarlet, her brown hair flowing wildly in the breeze from outside. She appeared to freeze when she saw me standing there, and I did the same when I laid my eyes upon her. I froze not because I thought she was beautiful, or because I was confused as to why this girl was standing in my home.

I froze because her lips were stained with blood.

Logically, I probably shouldn't have jumped to the conclusion that I did, and to this day I'm not sure how, but as soon as I saw her I *knew*. I did not ask her name, nor did I ask why she was here, or where she had come from. When I opened my mouth to speak to her, the words that escaped were, "What have you done with my mother?"

She didn't answer, instead a slow smile spread across her blood stained lips. And swaying slightly, she moved towards me. I took a step back, my eyes darting around the room in an attempt to find a weapon with which I could fend her off.

"Jamie?"

I froze when I heard her address me, using the nickname that only my mother used. Looking her over slowly, I attempted to gauge whether I knew her or not. And when my eyes settled on hers I knew that I had never seen this girl before, though she smiled at me fondly as though she knew me intimately. She reached out and I flinched away as her hand touched my face. "You look just like him," she said with a smile.

I swallowed hard, my throat suddenly dry from fear. This girl had killed my father, and I knew that soon enough I would be joining him in death. I asked once more, "What have you done with my mother?"

Again she ignored my question and instead stood on her toes, leaning her body into mine as though she were about to kiss me. "But you're not like him, are you?" she said with a smile. "Because you won't ever leave me."

I do not know what happened next, because everything went dark.

*

I kept my eyes shut tightly, feigning unconsciousness for as long as I was able. Too fearful of what may happen if I were to open my eyes. I had been awake for what felt like several hours and yet I lay unmoving, ignoring the whispers in my head that told me to get up and open my eyes.

"He is a stubborn one," I heard a man say. I noticed that he spoke with an accent and briefly I wondered if I was even in

England anymore.

The girl who lay beside me sighed, clutching at me as though I were some form of lifeless doll. "He doesn't want to play with me . . . Aleczander," she said. "Have you ever had someone ignore you like this?"

The man named Aleczander laughed slightly. "No," he said, his tone amused. "The boy must have a powerful will to resist your urgings."

"Maybe if he would open his eyes . . . " she said.

I forced my eyes to shut tighter and I heard her sigh in defeat and the man let out a chuckle. "Perhaps you should let him go."

"I can't let him go," the girl said. "I'm supposed to kill him."

For a moment there was silence. Briefly I wondered if the man had gone and I felt dread at the thought of being left alone with this girl once more.

"Who told you to kill him?" he asked, his voice sounding soft. "And why would you want to?"

"Look at his face!" she screamed. "He looks just like him!"

Aleczander sighed, and suddenly his voice was right beside me. "Victoria," he said softly. "This boy has done nothing to you. Just because the other hurt you . . . it is not *his* fault."

It wasn't until Victoria sniffed that I realised she must be crying. And some part of me felt that I should make some effort to comfort her, but when my mind recollected what she had done to my father I flinched at the thought of her being so close to me.

"It doesn't matter," she mumbled. I felt the mattress sink as she stood on the bed and climbed over me, though I did not hear her feet as they touched the ground. "It's too late . . . I have until tonight to put him with the others."

"Others?" Aleczander asked, his voice sounding alarmed.

Victoria let a sigh. "I already killed the rest of the household . . . he's the last one left."

I felt myself flinch at hearing her speak those words. My heart racing in my chest as my mind told me that the words she spoke couldn't possibly be true.

"Victoria," Aleczander called. "Victoria!"

I didn't know she had left until I heard the door slam shut.

"You can open your eyes if you wish," Aleczander said. "She is gone."

Slowly I opened my eyes. I was lying in a bed, wrapped up in duvet made of cream silk. The walls appeared to be made of a red stone and the room was filled with furniture in a French style that looked as though it were centuries old. My clothes lay in a pile on the far side of the room.

I let a sigh of relief when I saw that Victoria had in fact left the room.

"Do you know how long it will be before she comes back?" I asked, looking at Aleczander for the first time. He looked about my age, or perhaps a few years older. The age my brother would have been if he had been alive. His skin was pale, without a single freckle, as though he hadn't seen the sun for years. And once again, without having to ask, I *knew* what he was. I let a gasp and sat up, pushing myself back to put distance between us.

He watched me curiously, then seated himself on the edge of the bed. "If I had any intention of harming you, you would already be dead."

Without another word he rolled up his sleeve, never taking his eyes from my face as he watched me, his gaze assessing in its purpose. "What are you doing?" I asked, as I witnessed him raise his arm to his lips and bite down.

"Opening a wound," he stated matter-of-factly.

He held his now bleeding wrist out to me, and I stared at it momentarily, wondering what it was he expected me to do.

"Drink," he ordered.

I gazed at him dumbfounded, wondering if he was being serious or if he was playing some kind of practical joke.

I shook my head. "I don't understand."

Aleczander let an impatient sigh. "I have not the time for this . . . you do not *need* to die, now drink!"

At the time I was unsure as to why I complied with his demand, but looking back on it I now realise that he had probably used his Powers on me. Put me under some kind of Vampire glamour that compelled me to do as he ordered.

I remember the taste of his blood so clearly. I remember that my first feeling had been confusion, for I hadn't ever considered that blood would have a taste.

But it did.

At first it was metallic, like my mouth was filled with copper pennies, but after some time, the taste grew sweet and I began to crave it. Swallowing it eagerly down in gulps. My memories stop when Aleczander prised his wrist from me, for I swiftly fell into unconsciousness. The last human memory I have is the face of the Vampire who Turned me.

" . . . then what happened?"

Jamie looked to Sam curiously, the sound of her voice snapping him out of his memories. He opened his mouth to speak but paused when he saw what she held in her hand. "Where did you get that from?" he asked.

She smiled and took another bite of her chocolate bar. "Conjured it," she said. "I can't have stories without candy . . . it's just not how I roll." She waved the bar in front of his face. "Want some?"

Jamie shook his head, wondering how she could have

conjured something without him noticing. "Anyway . . . after that I woke up at home in the stables. I was surrounded by the mutilated bodies of the entire household . . . I assumed they were all left there to be found by the police, who I've since found out arrived in the morning. But when I saw the bodies of both my parents, I—"

"You freaked out?" Sam finished, taking another bite of her chocolate. "Anyone would have."

Jamie nodded his head. "Once I woke up, I wasn't going to stay there. I knew that with me being alive and everyone else dead I would have been blamed, so I burned the house down. Only taking the suitcase I had packed for university. And I ran."

"Wow," Sam said through a mouthful of chocolate. "I think that was a bit over the top . . . the whole burning it down thing. You should probably talk to a shrink, because fire-starting is a sign of crazy people."

"At the time it seemed perfectly logical," he said thoughtfully. "But a few years later there were some things that I wished I could've had that I would have been able to go back for had I not completely destroyed the house."

"You weren't thinking straight, I guess," Sam said with a shrug. "I've heard that when Vampires first Turn they go a bit psychotic before they fully adjust and become their normal selves again."

"I was back to my regular self, more or less, by the next day."

Sam raised an eyebrow and looked at him sceptically. "The next day?" she asked. "No, the psychotic stage lasts for at least a few months, and it's been known to go on for years for those who have no one to guide them. You were crazy 'til you met me . . . admit it."

Jamie laughed slightly. "I was fine by the next day," he

repeated. "Honestly, I was."

"Hmm . . . " she watched him assessing for a moment. "That's weird . . . maybe you're just naturally psychotic."

"I am *not* psychotic," he said defensively.

"You *did* blow up half of the school last week . . . I think that counts."

"You were in on that plan . . . What does that make you?"

Sam smiled slowly. "It was a hostage situation."

Jamie couldn't help laughing at her. "Liar," he said. "Everyone knows you're the ringleader."

Sam smiled. "So, anything else interesting happen?"

Jamie shrugged. "Not really. I spent the first year with Bethany." He looked in Sam's direction. "I met her the day after I was Turned. She was injured and I gave her some of my blood to heal her, but it Turned her instead. We got married, moved to Germany—"

"Why Germany?" Sam asked curiously.

Jamie smiled slightly. "I thought I would be able to find Aleczander there."

Sam nodded. "Makes sense I guess, that is where he's from."

"After a year we were attacked and she was killed."

Sam squinted her eyes in confusion. "If she was killed then how exactly did she end up here?"

Jamie let a sigh. "That's what I asked her. She didn't reply."

"Well . . . *that* doesn't sound suspicious at all." Sam's tone was completely sarcastic. For a moment, Jamie felt angry at her for jumping to the conclusion that Bethany was up to no good. But that feeling subsided after he realised that he'd thought the exact same thing.

And Bethany was doing herself no favours by refusing to answer his questions.

CHAPTER 9

$\mathcal{J}$amie opened the front door as stealthily as he could, feeling irritated by the fact that he felt it necessary to sneak into his own home. He peered into the living room from the doorway, only one foot inside the house, the other out on the porch.

Bethany was still unconscious on his sofa.

Carefully, he stepped inside, closing the door silently behind him. She stirred but didn't wake. With a sigh Jamie walked through the living room and up the stairs to his bedroom. The day had felt so long and right now all he wanted to do was crawl into his bed and sleep from this night to the next.

When Jamie next opened his eyes he was locked in a cell.

He jumped to his feet, the chains that encircled his wrists and ankles rattling with the sudden movement. Through the barred window on the door he saw the guard turn to gaze at him curiously once more. "Where is she!" Jamie shouted, his voice sounding foreign to his own ears.

The guard continued to stare.

Jamie pulled on the chains with all of his strength, willing them to break, but they didn't. His mortal strength wasn't enough to fight against the runes that were etched upon each of the links that bound him.

The door opened slowly and a girl walked in. She was slight in appearance and she gazed at him with curiosity, the same way everyone here seemed to look at him. In her hand she carried a vial, and he knew that it contained a potion that would put him into a state of slumber. The guard who watched his cell stepped forward, with another trailing in behind. They each grabbed onto his arms, restraining him, one of them knotting their hand in his hair to pull his head back so the girl could pour the potion into his mouth.

As soon as the vial was empty, Jamie spat the contents out, feeling no remorse as the potion stained the girl's dress. Again he yelled, "Where is she!"

The girl looked stunned and slightly fearful as she looked to the guards. "There's no time to get another," she said. "They want him in there now."

"It's alright," one of the guards said. "Run along."

The girl left without question.

One of the guards let Jamie go and bent to remove the chains from the hooks that fastened them to the stone floors. As soon as the chains were unclasped, he pulled away from the man that held him, throwing his elbow back in an attempt to fight him off.

Both guards grabbed him, holding on tightly as they dragged him forward, his chains rattling across the floor as he struggled with all of his strength to escape.

It was no use. He couldn't break free, but that didn't mean he would make their jobs simple.

"Tell me where she is!"

They did not answer him, pulling him down a long and narrow hallway.

The doors at the end of the hallway opened to reveal a grand hall filled with people — or *were* they people?

He felt his heart pound quickly as he saw her, unconscious and tied to a stake in the centre of the room.

"Samantha," he whispered.

"Don't!" he cried, briefly turning his head in the direction of the three Witches who sat upon their thrones. They regarded him with distaste, obviously feeling no compassion for him or his beloved. He tried to rush forward, propelling himself away from his guards, but they simply pulled on his chains to hold him back. "Don't hurt her!" he pleaded once more. "*Please!* She's done nothing to you!"

"Why has he not been spelled into silence?" asked one of the Witches, her voice sounding bored and uncaring.

Jamie struggled for freedom, not that anyone seemed to notice.

"He spat the potion out," one of the guards replied. "We couldn't get him to keep it down."

With a wave of her hand, the Witch sent a current of energy in his direction. Jamie felt the release of Power despite the fact that he was only human, and his body suddenly became heavy as the Witch's spell wrapped around him.

The last thing he saw before the flames consumed him were the Shadows that filled the room.

Jamie woke with a start, gasping despite the fact that he needed no air.

As his eyes adjusted to the room around him, he calmed. Realising that the dream, despite its vividness, had not been real.

"What's wrong?"

He jumped at the sound of Bethany's voice and turned his head, only now noticing her sitting on the edge of his bed. Briefly he wondered how long she'd been there. "Nothing," he replied. "Just a dream."

"Seemed more like a nightmare," she said, watching him carefully.

Slowly, he nodded his head.

She moved closer, her proximity making him shift uncomfortably. "You made me sleep."

"Yes," he replied simply.

She smiled. "You're a lot stronger than I remember."

He shrugged.

Bethany watched him for a few more moments before turning her attention to the window, where Jamie had left the curtains open. Outside the sky was turning from dark navy to a murky grey. "It's almost morning," she said, turning back to him with a smile on her face. "Do you mind if I join you?"

Jamie looked towards the clock on the table beside his bed. According to the glowing letters it was six-fifteen. He pushed the duvet off himself as he stood, getting out of the bed. "The bed is all yours," he said, fully aware that she was watching him, confused as to why she had been rejected. "I have to leave soon anyway."

"Leave?"

Jamie nodded, walking to the windows where he closed the curtains, sure that not a single beam of light would find its way through. "Yes," he replied, moving to the wardrobe for a change of clothes. "I have plans."

Bethany stood and drew close. "Could I come with you?"

"You can't," he said. "It will be daylight soon."

"If you could tell me how you go out, I could —"

"No," he said, turning to face her. She seemed startled, and again he wondered if he was really all that different from the person she remembered.

"You don't want me to come with you?"

He could tell by the look in her eyes that she was hoping he would say he *did* want her to come along. Somewhere deep inside he felt that he should do the polite thing and give her some form of explanation that would make her feel content and not completely rejected. But he hadn't the time or the patience to come up with a lie, so instead he told her the truth.

"I don't want you here," he said bluntly. "You're welcome to stay for a few days until you decide where you're moving on to next, but until then I'll stay out of your way and you stay out of mine."

"Jamie!"

He leaned forward so that their eyes were level, briefly thinking of the difference between her and Sam.

Sam was tall for a girl, so there wasn't much height difference between them. Bethany however, was an average female height, meaning Jamie had to bend to her, which was irritating. "*What?*"

She stood and stared at him, her mouth open slightly. She seemed offended, not that she *really* had any reason to be.

"What's wrong with you?"

Jamie stood straight and rolled his eyes. "There's nothing wrong with me," he replied. "I'm the same as I've always been, and I'm bored of this conversation."

She opened her mouth to respond, but Jamie didn't give her a chance. He placed his hand on her head and sent a bolt of Power into her body, causing her to lose consciousness once more.

As he lowered her to the bed a small part of him felt guilty for how he'd treated her, but if he was being honest with himself, the guilt wasn't enough to fight through his apathy.

CHAPTER 10

*J*amie opened his front door, startled to find Sam on the other side. He froze, looking over his shoulder as he took a moment to think of Bethany unconscious on his bed, and wondered briefly what Sam would think if she knew that he had incapacitated her, not once, but twice in the past twenty-four hours.

Quickly, he regained his composure, closing the door behind him.

"What are you doing here?" he asked, as he pulled his coat on. "I was on my way to meet you."

"It's raining," Sam stated, pushing herself away from the wall next to the front door.

Jamie looked towards the trees from the safety of the shelter that covered the porch of his house. He tilted his head slightly as he regarded the falling drops of water, only noticing the weather for the first time since he awoke. "So it is. That doesn't explain why you're here."

Sam rolled her eyes, as though she believed her actions needed no explanation. "I drive when it rains," she replied, as though the answer had been obvious. "And I figured you'd rather not walk around dripping water all day."

Jamie looked around the clearing that surrounded his home. Not finding any car, or evidence that Sam had driven to meet him. "Are you suggesting that we drive through a heavily wooded area? Because that doesn't sound very safe."

She laughed slightly. "No . . . " With a smirk she reached her hand *through* the wall of his house. "Get in," she said, directing towards the portal with a nod of her head.

With a groan, Jamie obliged, knowing that she was right; he *didn't* want to spend the entire day soaking wet.

Sam watched Jamie closely as he stepped through the portal.

Something seemed off with him today, but she couldn't quite figure out what it was. Perhaps he simply wasn't a morning person. Which would be completely understandable given what he was biologically. As far as she knew, there weren't any nocturnal creatures that *did* enjoy the morning time.

She followed him through the portal which left them standing inside her garage by the door. Jamie stood unmoving, looking at the car with a strange expression on his face. He appeared to be miles away, lost somewhere deep in thought.

Sam took the keys from her pocket and held them in front of his face, jingling them slightly to get his attention. "You can drive if you want," she said, thinking that perhaps it would cheer him up.

Though judging by the expression of horror he wore as he regarded her car keys, she had been wrong in her assessment.

"Are you completely mad?" he asked, though the question sounded rhetorical.

Sam lowered her hand, still holding her keys, and shrugged nonchalantly. "No need for name calling, I was just trying to cheer you up. Your sulky face is ruining my Friday."

Jamie sighed loudly. "I can't drive, *remember*? Having me do so would only be wise if you *want* to die in a horrible explosion."

"I don't think you can make the car explode just by not knowing how to drive it."

He shook his head, his shoulders slumped forward slightly. "I'm sure I could find a way," he mumbled.

Sam walked towards her car — which today looked the same shade of silver it was when she drove it to school — and opened the door, climbing inside. Jamie followed her lead and climbed into the front passenger seat, hugging his bag on his lap as he stared out the window, chin on hand, elbow on window frame. Lost in thought once more.

"Okay." Sam started the car, pressing the button on the garage door opener. "Why do you have a sulky face?"

Jamie shrugged. "I'm not sulking, I'm just thinking."

"About what?"

He shrugged again. "Nothing, it's just a dream I keep having. It's . . . *weird*. I always wake up feeling strange."

Sam was about to ask for more details, but he sighed loudly and smiled, his mood appearing to brighten as he turned to look in her direction. "It was just a dream though, so it's nothing to think too hard about I suppose."

CHAPTER 11

$\mathcal{J}$ade sat alone on Sam's couch, mindlessly flicking through the channels, not staying on one for long enough to even get a glimpse of whatever shows were airing.

Sam and Jamie were out, doing the whole school thing. Jack was out doing whatever it was Jack did, and she had no idea where Danny had disappeared to.

She let a sigh as she settled on some early noon cartoons, wishing she hadn't decided to take the year off before starting college. The only reason she'd done it was to stay with her mom after her dad had left. But now . . . Hayley was nowhere to be found and it wasn't as though she had really *needed* Jade around to begin with.

Jade left the remote on the couch and stood, stretching her arms above her head as she yawned. With a sigh she turned and walked into the kitchen.

Pausing in the doorway when she saw a man in the back yard.

Slowly, Jade backed out of the kitchen and ran up the stairs to Danny's room, knowing that he had a baseball bat lying around his room somewhere.

She hurried through the door, grateful for the fact that no one in this house believed in locks, and ran to his bed. Kneeling down on the floor and lifting up the duvet to peer underneath, Jade smiled and let a sigh of relief when she saw the metallic bat under there, wedged between boxes that she didn't take the time to look inside of.

She grabbed hold of the bat and stood, squeezing it tightly in her hand for a moment to adjust to the feel of it. She was about to make her way down the stairs to scare the man off when she froze, suddenly wondering if this man was even human. This was Sam's house after all, this intruder could be a Warlock or a Witch or something else . . .

Nervously, she gazed towards the bedroom window. From where she stood she couldn't see him, and she didn't want to move closer in case he saw her.

She ran down the stairs and grabbed the phone in the hallway, quickly scrolling through the contacts saved into its memory to find Sam's number. When she did, she pressed dial and waited, chewing her lip impatiently as she eyed the kitchen door. After a few seconds of ringing, she sighed and hung up. Then, scrolling through the list once more, found Danny's number and tried him instead.

He picked up the phone almost immediately. "Hello?"

Jade let a relieved sigh. "Oh thank God *someone* knows how to answer the phone."

He laughed. "What happened?"

"There's some guy skulking around outside . . . I—"

"Do you know him?"

Jade rolled her eyes. "If I knew him I wouldn't be calling, would I? I need to know if Sam has anything ready-made I can throw if he's not human."

Danny paused for a moment. "I'm coming home now, just stay inside the house and you'll be fine . . . He can't get in."

"I have a bat in case he's human," Jade said. "But if he's not, I'd feel better having something for that too."

"Okay, go to the attic, she keeps all the ready-made stuff there."

"Hold on." Jade ran back up the steps, then down the hall and up the second flight of stairs to the attic. "Where am I looking?"

"There should be a bunch of little glass vials on a shelf."

Jade scanned the room quickly, paying particular attention to the shelves, and smiled when she found one filled with small coloured glasses. "Found it."

"There should be a blue one . . . um, the bright blue one, I think."

Jade stared at the various shades of blue liquid. "Bright blue?"

"Um, more like neon . . . like strobe light blue."

She smiled again. "Got it."

"The glass breaks easily, so try not to get it on yourself."

"So, I just throw it?"

"Yeah . . . but *don't* go outside. I'll be home in a couple of minutes, just wait for me."

Danny hung up first and Jade stood with the phone in her hand, staring at the blue potion in front of her, chewing her lip as she decided whether or not she should take Danny's advice and stay put, or if she should just open a window and throw the potion out. With a sigh, she plucked one of the vials off the shelf and held it in her hand, careful not to hold on too tightly. She left the attic slowly, half hoping that the man would be gone by the time she got back to the kitchen.

He wasn't.

By the time she came back downstairs he was standing in the back yard, facing the kitchen window, looking right into the house. Jade froze by the fridge and he smiled widely, in an almost friendly manner, waving at her as if they were best friends.

Jade glared and pointed the bat at him, raising the vial in her hand to show him that she was prepared to attack. He gazed at the potion curiously.

"Can you hear me?" she asked.

Slowly, he nodded his head.

"Good." She took a step towards the window. "Back the fuck up and get out of here, you're trespassing and I have the legal right to kill you."

He squinted his eyes and tilted his head slightly, then opened his mouth, making it look like he was answering her though she couldn't hear a word he said. With an irate huff she stormed to the back door and flung it open, careful not to step outside where she knew she would be vulnerable.

"What?"

The man smiled, before repeating his words in a heavily accented voice. "I said, I don't think you can *legally* kill me. I'd have to be inside the house for you to not get arrested for that."

"Ha, ha," Jade said sarcastically. She pointed the bat at him again. "What are you doing here?"

"Um." He looked over his shoulder. "I'm here for the coven meeting. It was supposed to be on Monday, then it was moved to this morning, but Hayley doesn't seem to be home."

Jade lowered the bat slightly, eyeing the man suspiciously. "You're a dude, what are you doing in a Witch coven?"

He laughed slightly. "I am indeed a *dude*, does that mean I can't also be a Witch?"

Jade shrugged. "I dunno . . . I don't pay attention when

people go on about that stuff. *Anyway,*" she pointed the bat at him once more, "what are you doing *here,* at *this* house?"

He eyed the bat with amusement, placing his hands in his pockets before he replied. "I sensed Power in this direction, thought maybe the meeting had been moved."

"There is no meeting," Jade replied, watching the man carefully. Something about him didn't seem right. She had never spent any time around Hayley's coven, so she didn't know everyone who participated, but she was pretty sure this guy wasn't one of them. "Get lost," she said, raising the hand that held the potion. "Before I kill you."

"You wouldn't kill me," he said, taking a step towards her as if that would prove his point.

"Try me," she said through her teeth. "I've had a pretty rough week, and I'm at the stage where I don't trust anyone, so *stranger,* you have 'til five to fuck off . . . One . . . "

He stood there.

"Two . . . "

He smiled.

"*Three . . .* "

He laughed slightly.

"Fo —"

"Jade!" She turned curiously, peeking her head out slightly as she saw Madison hop the fence that separated her back yard from Sam's and run towards her. "Don't!"

Jade lowered the potion. "You know this guy?"

"Five," he said with a smirk. "And look . . . I'm not dead."

Jade shot him a glare.

Madison rolled her eyes at him, not that he seemed to notice. "Yeah," she said. "He's —"

"A coven member," he cut in. "Just as I said."

"Is that true?" Jade asked, turning her attention to Madison. "Blink twice if he's evil, I've been told to throw this if he starts anything."

Madison laughed slightly. "He's not evil," she said.

"Hmm . . . " Jade regarded the man for a moment, before turning her attention back to Madison. "Hayley's fucked off somewhere, don't know when she'll be back so call everyone and tell them not to bother showing up for whatever meetings are planned."

CHAPTER 12

ithout another word she slammed the door in their
faces, which Malachi thought was incredibly rude.

"Are you *insane*?" Madison hissed. "Seriously, if I hadn't
sensed you hanging around here you could have been *killed*."

"She wasn't going to kill me," Malachi replied, watching
through the window as the girl walked through the kitchen,
not looking back at him even once, which was more than a
little disappointing.

Madison raised her hand to clip him over the head, but he
moved—his reflexes faster than hers—and she missed,
stumbling forward slightly when her palm made no impact.
She recovered quickly and turned on him, glaring as she did.
Grabbing hold of his sleeve, she pulled at his arm. He allowed
her to pull him away from the window and out of sight.
"What if Sam had been home?" she asked as they walked to
the front of the house and out onto the street.

Malachi shrugged. "Then I would fight her, and hopefully

I'd win."

Madison gaped at him. "You plan to kill her?"

He stared at her, clenching his jaw as he tried to suppress the rage that was stirring within him. With forced calm he said, "She killed Kraven, for that she must die."

Madison followed closely as Malachi stormed down the street, seeming more enraged now than he had before. It seemed that with every step he took his anger increased. At least that's how it looked to Madison as she watched him walk with an almost march-like step, clenching and unclenching his fists by his sides. As he began to walk in the direction of the high school, she reached out and grabbed onto his arm, the fabric of his coat clenched in her hand, causing him to stop when the sleeve began to pull from his shoulder.

"What?" he asked through gritted teeth, turning to her swiftly, as though her mere presence was nothing more than an irritation.

"Calm down," she ordered, ignoring the hurt that bubbled up inside her as she could do nothing but watch as he glared at her with such hatred.

She felt the hate was directed towards her, even though somewhere in her mind she knew it was not.

He stared at her for a moment, his blue eyes blazing with the Power that lived within him, almost glowing with the fury she knew he felt. Then, after a moment, he let his lids drift shut, and took a breath, his shoulders relaxing as he exhaled. "She needs to die," he said calmly without opening his eyes to look at her.

Madison let her hand fall from his arm and stared up at the sky where there was nothing but grey, the clouds fat with the rain they were sure to expel today.

"Did you hear me?" he asked, opening his eyes to stare at her; his pupils dilated and wild. "I said —"

"I *heard* you," she replied, cutting him off before he had a chance to repeat himself. "Sam is a *child* Malachi, do you understand that? A child. She doesn't understand the situation, she doesn't understand her *part* in the situation. What she did was wrong, but she only did it because she doesn't understand."

"How can you —"

"*You* weren't there . . . *I* wasn't there. Neither of us knows what happened, but we both know Sam and how she operates. She doesn't attack first."

"But Kraven wouldn't have attacked her!" he yelled, his tone desperate, his pale face flushed with colour, his eyes pleading for understanding. "He wouldn't have done that. You didn't know him like I did, and he wouldn't . . . he just wouldn't have gone behind my back like that."

Madison sighed, looking at Malachi with pity. The man had been alive since the eighteen hundreds, yet still, he idolised Kraven and was subsequently unable to see the flaws in his own memories.

"Malachi," she said, placing a hand on his shoulder. "I think you're the one who didn't really know him."

His shoulders sagged as he looked at her with eyes that were close to tears. "But . . . I loved him," his voice was barely a whisper. "And she *murdered* him."

"Go home," she said, her tone kind yet firm. "You haven't slept in days, you need to rest. We can make a plan later. Just get some sleep, okay?"

Slowly, he nodded his head, staring down at the ground with a despondent expression. It was then that Madison realised, that despite his age, in his grief he too was just a child.

A child who'd lost the only person in the world he loved.

CHAPTER 13

*T*he house looked the same as every other house.

All of the people around it seemed to be getting on with their lives as though nothing had actually happened. There was a moment when Jack considered asking one of the neighbours if they had any ideas about what had happened to the people who lived there. The man, the woman and their son, who these people wouldn't have seen in almost a week.

He didn't bother asking though, because he had the strangest feeling that they wouldn't have anything to say to him. And once again he sighed as he stared at the house that was so tainted by evil he could feel it from his perch on the rooftop of the home across.

Something wasn't right.

Jack had spent a full weekend watching that house, and he *knew* that he saw something important. Something had happened, but for some reason he couldn't remember. Like so many other things that seemed to be missing from his memories.

He thought of what Jamie had said to him, on the roof of Sam's house over a week ago, and he frowned at the memory, taking a hand and placing it over his heart as he took a deep breath and concentrated.

Beneath his fingers his heart beat steadily. He closed his eyes and clenched his jaw. Forcing the memories to come and fill the gaps in his mind.

It was dark and Jack sat on his rooftop perch watching the house carefully. It had been quiet for most of the day, ever since both of the parents returned home. Time seemed to move slowly as he waited for the boy to return, it had taken hours and was past two a.m. before he strolled home, appearing drunk in his movements. The boy didn't seem to sense him as he walked into the house.

Jack stood, waiting for a light to go on in one of the rooms.

Nothing happened for a few minutes.

Jack jumped from the roof he was perched on and landed in the front garden, walking slowly towards the house.

The garage door opened, and Jack looked on curiously as the boy drove a car out, turning his head in Jack's direction as he seemed to register his presence. His lips curled back, showing his teeth and he drove at Jack, attempting to run him over.

Jack dematerialised before the car hit.

He rematerialized inside the garage, peeking out the door as he watched the car speed off.

With a sigh, Jack turned, looking towards the door that led to the house. He walked forward, letting himself inside, curious to see what had caused the boy to leave so quickly.

Jack's breath caught in his throat as he saw the bloody footprints that stained the floor. He stepped into the house, and followed the trail to their source. They ended in front of a door that was still open. Slowly, Jack reached forward and pulled it open all the way, walking forward and –

"Jack."

Jack opened his eyes, and slowly looked towards the man who had spoken.

He smiled his mocking smile, and Jack clenched and unclenched his fist, only now remembering the man and how much he despised him.

"Shino," he spat the name as though it was a disease.

He just smiled in return. "Why do you constantly insist on not doing as you're told?"

Jack stood. "Because you're going to get Sam killed!"

Shino laughed as though he found that amusing. He reached out and placed his hand on Jack's head, sending a current of energy rushing through him, causing his muscles to spasm and ache as they slowly became numbed. "I know," he said as Jack fell to his knees. "That's the point."

CHAPTER 14

After calling ahead to Lucy, the newest of Malachi's recruits, Madison brought him to her house and allowed him use of the portal to travel home. Lucy would be waiting to escort him to his room. Madison had given strict orders for the other woman to ensure that he got some rest and she hoped—despite the fact that she wasn't officially anything in rank—her command would be obeyed.

Once Malachi had vanished through the sheen of energy, she let a long, heavy sigh and rested her forehead against the hallway wall. Rubbing her eyes which felt suddenly heavy, as though she also needed sleep.

"Why are you not in school?"

Madison jumped, turning around sharply to face the kitchen, where she only now noticed her father sitting at the table, flicking through the newspaper.

She pushed herself away from the wall and walked over to him, taking a seat on one of the wooden chairs that surrounded the table. "Why are you not in work?"

He raised his head from behind the paper and looked at her. She could tell that he was smiling despite the fact that she could only see the top half of his face. "After the break-in we had, I've decided to stay home for a while. And you're not in school because . . . "

"I found the idiot lurking in Sam's backyard on the way, thought it would be best to make sure he doesn't kill her, or draw attention to everyone by being stupid."

The paper hit the table, and now her dad's smile was visible. He seemed amused by her words, not that Madison was sure why.

She leaned back in her chair and looked out through the hallway. "Where's Joyce?"

Her father sighed and shrugged. "Out somewhere," he said. "Probably shopping, maybe at a friend's house. She didn't tell and I didn't ask."

"Problems?"

"She's tired," he stated, as if that statement was all the explanation that Madison would need.

Her stepmother was a simple woman—a human woman— who wanted nothing more from life than a house, a family and enough money that she didn't have to worry about finances. She loved Madison's father because he provided her with two of the three things she desired.

"She wants kids?"

He laughed a little. "Among other things, yes."

Madison stood and walked over to the counter, pouring them both a cup of coffee. She placed one in front of her dad and kept the other for herself. Sitting back down, she asked, "What other things?"

"It's her birthday in a few weeks," he began, sipping coffee from his cup. "She'll be thirty. I think it's starting to get to her.

The fact that she's aging and I'm not. She asked if there was a way for me to become human, so that we could grow old together. I explained to her that that would involve me giving up the job I've had for over a millennia, giving up the Magic I was born with and the life I'm accustomed to and then spend the few years of life I'd have before my death as a human struggling to adjust to my new life. It wasn't a practical or reasonable request for her to make . . . she knew I wouldn't do any of that when we married. I think she has regrets and doesn't want to have any more of them. It's likely we'll divorce, which is a shame. I was just starting to get attached to this one."

Joyce was his seventh wife in over three centuries. He'd had so many girlfriends that Madison had completely lost count. The only ones that she ever paid any attention to, or ever bothered getting to know were the ones that her father cared enough about to marry.

But all of his wives left him eventually, no longer able to cope with the fact that they would age and he would not. Eventually they realised that they were wasting their lives with a man who would never fully commit to them.

A man who would never teach them Magic and make them immortal to spend an eternity with them, and a man who would never relinquish his immortality to grow old with them.

"Why not teach her some Magic and see if she can get strong enough to become immortal with you?" This was always Madison's suggestion, despite the fact that she knew what his answer would be she always made a point of saying it. Just to remind him that there was an option other than death or divorce.

"I've only been married to her for eight years . . . I'll probably get bored after fifty, if it even takes that long, and then we'll divorce but I'll still be responsible for her as her mentor."

Madison sighed in irritation. "Well, maybe you should stop marrying women you don't want to spend forever with."

"Forever is a long time. The only female I could bear to spend my life with is you, and that's only because of my paternal obligation to love you."

"You always say such kind things to me," Madison said sarcastically.

Her father was someone she had never quite gotten used to, which she supposed was strange given the fact that she'd been around him for her whole life.

He was a Warlock from birth, and although she knew the date of his birthday, October twelfth, she didn't know the exact year because he'd never told her. But she knew that he was one of the oldest Warlocks alive right now, which meant he was at least a little over a millennia old.

She'd never met her paternal grandparents, didn't know a thing about the woman who birthed her, and didn't know a thing about her father's life before she was born.

And she'd never asked about any of those things.

Either because she they weren't important to her, or because he'd influenced her to not dwell on questions he didn't want to answer.

The things she did know about him were that he liked what he was, enough that he'd been excited to teach her how to use her Powers when they'd started to manifest.

She knew that he was a high-ranking member of the Underworld. And Madison knew that he loved her enough to not ever involve her in his work.

She also knew that he was not happy when she'd gotten involved anyway.

Her father sighed, and quickly changed the subject,

glancing towards the wall in the hallway where the currently inactive portal was located. "You do realise that he's technically in charge now? I'm not quite sure you're allowed to refer to him as 'the idiot'."

She shrugged. "I'm sure it's fine."

He watched her carefully as he sipped his coffee. "If it's not you'll be jailed, at best."

Madison smiled. "I'll be expecting you to break me out then."

He laughed. "What else are fathers for if not breaking their daughters out of prison and beating any boys who get too close to them?"

Madison jumped to her feet. "That reminds me, I should go see how Scott is."

Her dad sighed. "I stand by what I said, I don't care if his father works for the police. I'll make it look like an accident. Car crash, fall from a cliff . . . eaten by wolves."

Madison scowled at her dad. "Why would you want to hurt Scott?"

"I don't want to hurt him as long as he stays away from you."

"Is it because he's human? Because that's a bit hypocritical don't you think?"

"Darling, I don't care in the slightest that he's human. What bothers me is the fact that he's male. It wouldn't matter if he was a Warlock, a Witch, a Lycanthrope, a Vampire or a genetically modified lab creature. If he's male he gets a beating. That's how life works."

With a roll of her eyes, she turned and walked out of the kitchen and towards the front door.

"Look both ways before crossing the street!" her dad yelled after her.

As Madison walked out of her house, she dwelled on her

father's relationship problems. Somewhat upset that she would most likely be losing another stepmother due to her father's stubbornness and refusal to compromise for the sake of his wife.

She shook her thoughts away and made her way across the street to Scott's house, looking both ways as her father requested despite the fact that the area was residential and there was no traffic to be seen. Arriving at the front door in less than twenty seconds, she walked up the driveway, noticing that there were no cars.

Madison hoped that he hadn't decided to show up to school today after being absent for most of the week. She knocked, and waited patiently for a response.

During the past few days she'd tried calling him on multiple occasions, but had gotten his voicemail every time. She'd been meaning to check in personally for a while, but had been distracted dealing with Malachi.

It took what felt like five minutes for anyone to answer the door.

Slowly, the door cracked open. On the other side was a very rough looking Scott. "Hi," he said, giving her a weak smile as he kept his eyes half closed against the light. His usually tanned skin looked pale, his hair was messy and his pyjamas creased, as though he'd been doing nothing but sleep for a good few days. He opened the door fully and stepped back, waving her inside. "Get in before the sunlight kills me."

Madison rolled her eyes and stepped inside the house shutting the door behind her. Scott turned and began making his way up the stairs, his bare feet hitting the steps heavily as he moved.

"You look like shit," Madison said as she followed him.

"Thanks," he croaked, before coughing to clear his throat. "You're so kind to me."

He led the way down the hall and into his room. Once she was inside he shut the door and stumbled to his bed, where he sat down with a heavy sigh, turning to her with a smile. "That's better."

"Why is it so dark in here?" she asked, looking around at the darkened room, knowing that if it wasn't for the glowing light—which was emanating from the TV—she wouldn't have been able to make out the shape of her own hands. She walked over to the curtains, planning to open them. "It's like a Vampire's lair in—"

Her words were cut off by the sound of Scott's screams. She turned quickly, her eyes wide with shock as she stared at him clutching his head as he doubled over, as though he was in an immense amount of pain.

She ran to him, placing a hand on his back in an attempt to comfort him.

He was breathing heavily as he stared at the ground, hands still clutching his head.

"What's wrong?" she asked. "Do you need some painkillers? Are you going to throw up?"

He shook his head, his hair falling down and completely obscuring his face from view. Madison knelt down beside him, brushing his hair back so she could get a better look at his face.

She noticed the blood before anything else.

A few drops flowing from his nose—looking black in the dark of the room—staining his face as he swayed slightly. The sight of it was enough to incite not only shock within her, but fear.

He looked forward, sitting upright as he wiped the blood from his nose, staring straight ahead with an unseeing expression.

"Scott?" she called, waving a hand in front of his face.

He was unresponsive, just staring into space, his eyes glazed over as though he was in a trance. She clicked her fingers a couple of times in an attempt to snap him out of it. It didn't seem to work, so she shook him. Hard.

With a startled jump, he blinked and stared at her, as if his brain was just registering her presence. "Sorry," he said with another weak smile. "Did you say something?"

Madison stared at him, assessing in her gaze. "I've been trying to call you, and text you," she said slowly.

He laughed a little before running a hand through his hair, brushing it away from his face. "Yeah . . . I lost my phone a couple of days ago. Not sure where though, I'll look when I'm feeling better."

She sighed and sat down beside him. "What's wrong with you anyway? Is it contagious?"

He shrugged. "I'm not really sure what's wrong. I've had this killer headache for, like," he took a moment to count on his fingertips, "three or four days . . . I think. It's getting better . . . slowly, but I guess that's better than nothing."

"You do realise your nose was bleeding, like five seconds ago, right? That doesn't sound good, have you seen a doctor? You might need to get checked out or something."

"My mom said it was fine, and she went to med school."

Madison gave Scott a sideways glance. "She's a shrink. I don't think she can really tell with medical stuff, can she?"

He shrugged again, then sighed, before he grabbed the TV remote from the bed and began twirling it around in his hands. "If I tell you something weird, do you promise not to have me committed?"

Madison looked at him for a moment, thinking that if he only knew what she was, he'd know that there wasn't a lot she found weird. At least not by human standards.

She nodded encouragingly.

He chewed his lower lip. "I think I was attacked . . ."

"Attacked? By—"

He put a hand over her mouth to silence her and shook his head. "I know that I'm gonna sound crazy, that I was probably drunk or something, but there was this woman, and I spent most of last weekend with her . . . at least I think I did, it's kinda fuzzy and I can't really remember, but I have this mark, and when I saw it, I remembered. And I think I was attacked . . . by a . . . Vampire . . . " He spoke the last word slowly and stared at her expectantly, awaiting her reaction. He let a sigh when she said nothing. "My headache gets worse when I think about . . . *Vampires* . . . " He let a shaky breath before continuing. "Do you think that she could have, like, erased my memories so that I wouldn't know? Can they do that? I'm not really into books or films about . . . *them*, so I don't know. Do you know? Can you Google it or something? Is that even something you *can* Google?"

Madison stayed silent. Just watching him, paying close attention to his neck where there were no bite marks. She wondered where exactly this mark was, and why—if he was attacked by a Vampire—she didn't get rid of all the marks.

Unless there were so many she forgot one.

Madison let a sigh, before asking the one question she couldn't *not* ask, unable to mask the bitterness in her tone as she spoke. "Why didn't you try to ask Sam about it? You know she just *loves* all of that supernatural stuff."

He stared at her, eyes squinted in confusion. "Why would I ask Sam? We don't talk anymore."

Madison felt her lips part as she stared at him, dumbfounded. "Are you kidding me?" she whispered. "No offense, but you're a borderline Sam stalker."

His cheeks flushed slightly with embarrassment. "Well . . . not anymore. I'm done with Sam. I'm open to friendship, but,

after everything . . . the feelings are just . . . " He sighed. "I just
don't feel anything for her anymore."

"You what?"

He shrugged and smiled. "It's weird, right? I'm not sure
when it happened, I just woke up this week completely over
her." His expression turned suddenly serious. "About what I
said though, do you believe me?"

Madison let a sigh, thinking that as far as she knew the only
Vampire in town was the one who followed Sam around. And
since she was sure *he* didn't take Scott for a weekend she
wasn't sure what to think. It wasn't completely ridiculous to
think that another one could be around, but surely she would
have showed up on *somebody's* radar. "Can I see the mark?"

His face burned a brighter shade of red. "No!"

Madison raised a confused eyebrow.

"It's in a *private* place . . . I'm not gonna *show* you. That
would be way too weird. You're a *girl*."

Nice of you to finally notice, she thought with a sigh. "Are you
kidding me? Is it really on your —"

"Yes," he cut her off. "Just take my word for it, okay?"

Madison watched him for a moment. Her lips quirked
slightly before she burst into a fit of laughter. Scott scowled at
her. "It's *not* funny."

His indignant expression only made her laugh harder.

He let a sigh of frustration, though she could tell that he
was trying not to laugh as well. "Do you think I'm crazy or
not?"

"Are you sure it's not like a bug bite, or a piercing . . . or an
STD?"

"I do *not* have an STD! Why would an STD look like fang
marks?"

"I don't know that it does look like fang marks," she said
with a smile. "How can I tell what it looks like if you won't let

me see?"

He sighed and looked away. "What do you know about . . . *them* anyway?"

Madison stared at the ceiling for a moment, attempting to judge how much she could say without giving away everyone's secrets. "Well, I know they can't go out in daylight or they'll burn."

Scott nodded his head. "Everyone knows that, what else? What about, like, mind control?"

"Um . . . well, there are some legends that would support their ability to, not really mind control, but persuade. Like they couldn't make you kill yourself because your instincts would kick in and not allow that to happen. But they could maybe make you do other, non-lethal things."

"So it's possible that I was mind controlled?"

" . . . What *exactly* happened?"

"I don't remember a lot, but it was mostly, um . . . sex things. And biting . . . I'm pretty sure she kept biting me, like, *everywhere*." He shivered slightly. "She kept asking me questions about . . . something . . . I think she was looking for—" He cut himself off with a groan and placed a hand to his head. "I can't think about it anymore."

Madison pressed her lips tightly. She had never spent any time around Vampires, so she didn't know what the signs of someone who was attacked would look like, but if she were to guess, she would say they'd look an awful lot like Scott did now.

CHAPTER 15

$\mathcal{L}$ucy greeted him on the other side of the portal. Malachi glared at her, instantly realising that she'd been told to await his arrival. He sighed. "Are you my babysitter now?"

She smiled guiltily and shrugged. "I was told to make sure you get to bed and sleep."

He rolled his eyes, but didn't move from his place by the portal, which was now inactive. "I do not need to be told what to do, I'm in charge here, or have you forgotten that already?"

She frowned at him and folded her arms across her chest.

Although it was correct that he was now in charge due to Kraven's death, there were many people, including some of the new recruits, who were having a difficult time seeing him as such. It was something that he didn't appreciate, given the amount of time and effort he had put in to the place and the people there. True, he wasn't the oldest member, but he had been the most valued.

At least in Kraven's eyes he had been.

"I'm not going to stay here where I'll probably be murdered in my sleep."

"What are you talking about?" Lucy asked, with a sigh of irritation. "No one is planning to kill you, although I am tempted to do it if it will stop your moping."

"I'm not moping!" he yelled. "I'm angry."

"Then do something about it," she said simply. "If the Witch makes you angry take her out of the picture. I am a firm believer in vengeance."

You would be, he thought with a sigh. Having a Vampire Hunter agree with his motives and his thoughts about the Witch was not comforting. With a scowl he turned from her and reopened the portal he had stepped through, using it to take him to Kraven's last known location.

"Where are you going?"

"I have things to do," he replied without turning to look in her direction.

"But . . . we still haven't talked about Bethany!"

With a sigh and a shake of his head, Malachi ignored her and stepped through the portal. He had more important things to consider than the ideas of vengeance manifested by Vampire bait.

CHAPTER 16

It was only fifteen minutes after Jade had gone inside that Danny barged through the front door. "Where is he?" he asked, storming into the living room where she was sitting on the couch. She watched him over her shoulder as he leered into the kitchen like a creep.

"Gone," Jade replied through a mouthful of popcorn. "I scared him off with my death threats."

With a sigh Danny let himself drop to the couch. He gazed at her as though he was about to reprimand her, but instead he smiled. "I told you not to do anything."

"No," she said as she held out her popcorn bowl, offering some to him. He declined with a shake of his head. "You told me not to go outside, which I didn't. I threatened him from the doorway."

Danny tutted and shook his head. "What did he want? Do you know who he is?"

Jade shook her head. "I don't know who he is, he said he

was looking for Hayley for the coven meeting, but I don't know if I believe that. Madison showed up and vouched for him though, so," she shrugged, "whatever."

"Madison?" Danny looked at her curiously for a moment, apparently thinking incredibly hard to place the name with a face.

"Redhead," Jade said. "Used to be friends with Sam, she's BFF's with Scott."

"Ah," Danny nodded and smiled. "I miss Scott, he was good people."

"I prefer the new guy," Jade replied.

Danny rolled his eyes.

She laughed. "You only hate him because he's a Vampire . . . you're racist against Vampires."

"No I'm not," he said defensively. "That's not the only reason I dislike him. He literally tried to kill Sam, and . . . he doesn't seem trustworthy is all."

Giving him a disbelieving look, Jade changed the subject. "Where were you anyway?"

He sat back on the couch, stretching his legs out in front of him. "Getting food," he said. "Sam's got the house stocked with junk. Has she *ever* bought actual groceries?"

Jade laughed. "I don't think so, she lives off take-out."

Danny shook his head and sighed. "I know she knows how to cook, we both learned, so why is she so fucking lazy?"

"You know, you could have just stolen all of the food from my house. It will probably go bad before Hayley shows her face again."

"You do have a point." He looked at her thoughtfully then stood. "You got keys?"

"No," Jade said following suit. "I forgot to grab them before a giant portal opened in the middle of my room and I was kidnapped by a crazy person."

"Hmm . . ."

He walked out of the living room and through the front door. Jade followed him outside, leaving the door open behind her.

"Are we actually stealing all the stuff from my house?" she asked as walked out into the street and onto her front lawn.

"Yeah," he replied, making his way to the front door. "I abandoned my shopping when you said the house was under attack, and besides, do you want the place to stink up the neighbourhood?"

Jade paused for a second, wrinkling her nose in disgust as she imagined what a kitchen full of rotten food would smell like. "Gross."

She jogged up to the door where Danny was now wiggling the handle, standing close to the door as he attempted to break the lock. He looked to Jade as she approached. "Cover me on this side."

Jade moved in closer, using her body as a shield so that anyone coming up the driveway or passing by on the street wouldn't be able to see the blue sparks that came from Danny's fingers and flowed into the lock on the door. After a few seconds, there was a click, and Danny moved his hand away with a triumphant smile on his face.

"I've seen more impressive Magic," Jade said.

He frowned and looked in her direction. "I never really practiced," he said defensively. "So excuse me if my talents are a bit rusty."

"Does it feel weird to use your Powers?" Jade asked curiously as he pushed the door open.

"No," he replied, his expression completely serious. "It feels perfectly natural . . . that's what bothers me."

Jade followed Danny over the threshold, half expecting to see Hayley walking out of the living room and feeling a tinge of longing for the old days, when her mother would greet her with a smile and not a glare.

Thinking back on how she had been in the past few weeks made Jade grateful for the fact that the house was still empty. The air in the house seemed electric and the fine hairs on the back of her neck stood on end. She exhaled as she gazed around the house . . . the building didn't feel like home.

Even Jade, with her non-supernatural senses could feel that the air was tainted.

"God," she whispered. "This place is so creepy."

Danny turned in her direction. "You can go back home if you want."

Home. Jade smiled slightly at his words, he spoke as though it was her home too. "Sadly," she said with a grim smile, "I am home."

Danny laughed slightly as he shut the door behind them, blocking the chill from the air outside. Not that the air inside was any warmer. "You live with us now," he said patting her on the shoulder in a sorry attempt at comfort. "You're practically part of the family."

"Thanks," Jade said, forcing a smile. "Though I honestly think your family is more fucked up than mine."

"You mean Sam," he stated, though Jade thought he probably should have spoken it as a question.

"She's my friend, but . . . I don't know if it's what she is, or if it's just her personality, there's just something not right with her. There hasn't been for a while."

"I don't know if there was ever a time when she *was* alright," Danny said as he looked around the hallway. "When she first came to us she was *damaged*, everyone thought over time she'd get better but . . . " he shrugged. "Maybe it *is* just what she is, though Jack seems to believe it's not *her* but how she was raised."

Jade let a sigh. "That's because Jack loves her and doesn't want to think there's anything that could possibly be wrong with *her*. If Sam finds my mom she'll kill her, and she won't even feel bad about it and I bet she'll still expect me to have her back."

Danny wrapped an arm around Jade's shoulder and squeezed her for a moment. "I promise you, I won't let Sam hurt your mom . . . we'll find her and we'll heal her, that's the plan."

Jade nodded her head, despite the fact she wasn't entirely convinced what he said was true. "Kitchen's that way," she said, pointing straight ahead to the door at the end of the hallway. "I'm gonna go get some stuff from my room."

Danny nodded. "Okay." Leaving Jade alone to ponder on her thoughts, he vanished through the door and as she walked up the stairs she wondered if she would even feel bad if her mom was killed.

Things had been bad right before Hayley had gone, she'd been acting weird, and she'd been getting violent. Jade was starting to feel as though she wasn't safe at home.

Though if the cause of that had been a magical one, then surely it wasn't really Hayley's fault . . . was it?

With a sigh, she opened the door to her bedroom, groaning internally as she saw what a mess it was. Papers littered her bed, where she'd been studying before she'd been taken, all of which had blood spattered on them.

Her blood.

Clothes were strewn about the floor, which they hadn't been beforehand. Drawers were open, with items spilling out. The room looked like someone had torn it apart in search of something. Though she wasn't sure what . . . as far as she knew she didn't have anything of value. At least, she didn't have anything that was of value to a Warlock.

She walked into her room, bending to gather up the items of clothing as she used her foot to kick the door shut behind her. She threw the bundle onto the desk in the corner of her room, deciding she'd rather not have her clothes touch off the blood stained sheets . . . even if the blood was no longer wet enough to contaminate her clothes.

Jade took a breath, closing her eyes momentarily as she blocked out memories of the last time she'd set foot into this room. When she opened her eyes she caught her reflection in the mirror on her wall. She looked as tired as she felt, dark circles shadowed her eyes, her hair was messy and desperately needed to be washed and her body looked thin in Sam's clothes, which were a size bigger than her own. With a sigh, she turned to her closet, grateful that she would be able to change into her own clothes for the first time in three days.

Just as she reached her closet, a gust of wind rushed past her, blowing her hair into her eyes. With a frown, she turned, not remembering the window being open.

Her lips parted and a scream escaped her as the wall by her bed shimmered and glowed, the tell-tale signs of a portal being opened. She rushed for the door, dropping the t-shirt she held in her hands, and grabbed onto the handle, attempting to tear the door open.

Arms wrapped around her waist, lifting her off her feet, and before she had a chance to escape, or fight, or even call for help, she was falling through the portal.

CHAPTER 17

$\mathcal{J}$amie let a heavy sigh as he sat down on the uncomfortable plastic chair. The cafeteria was more or less the same as it had been before the fire, except now the fumes of fresh paint clung to the air.

The stench made Jamie feel dizzy.

He placed a hand to his head as he nursed his growing headache and with a groan he reached into his bag and pulled out a flask. Uncapping it and gulping down more than half the contents in one go.

"You can't be *that* hungry," Sam said with a smile.

"I feel like I haven't eaten in days," Jamie said, fastidiously licking all traces of blood from his lips as he gazed around the immediate area to see if anyone was looking.

They weren't.

He turned his attention to Sam as he heard her sigh. When he looked at her he saw that she was glaring into the distance. He turned, following her line of sight towards the table nearest the door where the group of people — which usually included Scott — sat.

Jamie rolled his eyes and turned his attention back to Sam. "Get over it," he said harshly.

She looked at him, her eyebrows raised in an expression of surprise. "Wow," she said. "What's got your panties in a bunch?"

"What?"

"Why are you in a bad mood?" she clarified. "It's Friday. Friday's supposed to be a good mood day."

He sighed and rolled his eyes. "I'm not in a bad mood. Why does everyone keep thinking there's something wrong with me?"

"Everyone?" Sam raised an eyebrow. "Who else thinks you're in a bad mood?"

"Never mind," he mumbled, not wanting to start a conversation on Bethany and how he had been basically keeping her in a state of unconsciousness since she'd arrived.

"According to the whispers I've overheard, Scott's been absent since the last time we saw him," Sam said, her attention back on the group of students. Jamie groaned internally, he was sick of Sam's obsession over the mortal boy. "I was thinking —"

"I don't want to hear it," Jamie interrupted. "I'm not giving him his memories back."

"Not what I was going to say," Sam replied with a glare. "I was thinking about what he said happened last weekend."

Jamie finished off the contents of his flask, frowning as he found he was still hungry and wishing that he'd brought another. "What about the weekend?" he asked, only half paying attention to what she was saying.

"Scott said he was fed on by a Vampire, for an entire weekend."

"So?"

She rolled her eyes. "Well, doesn't it seem strange that after *that* another Vampire just happens to show up?"

"Bethany?" Jamie asked with a snort. "You think Bethany held Scott prisoner for a weekend?"

"Think about it," Sam said, leaning in closer. "It's the only thing that makes sense. Scott was fed on by a Vampire, and as far as I know *you* didn't do it and there's only one other Vampire in town, so obviously it was her."

Jamie shook his head. "I don't know if I believe that. It just doesn't seem like something she'd do."

"Kidnapping a guy and feeding on him over the weekend, and let's face it, probably raping him too, doesn't sound like the person you barely know and haven't seen in over a hundred and eighty years?"

Jamie let a sigh of defeat. "Alright, point taken. What do you expect *me* to do about it?"

For a brief, uncomfortable moment, Sam looked at him strangely. "Nothing," she replied. "There's nothing we can do about it, I'm just saying we should make sure it doesn't happen again."

"Vampires have to eat, Sam," he said, rolling his eyes and turning away, avoiding the watch of her scrutinising gaze. "If Bethany wants to feed on someone you can't stop her from eating . . . even if that someone is Scott."

"Scott is off limits!" Sam yelled, quickly looking around to ensure no one had heard her outburst.

They hadn't and they wouldn't.

Jamie had them both wrapped up in a bubble of energy that kept them practically invisible to everyone in the area. They could be killing each other or having sex on the table and no one would ever know.

With a sigh he dropped his empty flask into his bag, and,

never taking his eyes off Sam he leaned in across the table. "Stop obsessing," he said, knowing that he sounded harsh but not caring.

For a second time, she watched him strangely, and immediately he was reminded of their tryst the other night. He licked his lips as he watched her scowl at him, thinking of the various ways he could make her smile.

"I'm not obsessing," she said defensively. "I abandoned him to keep him out of this, and I don't like the idea of a Vampire waltzing in here and fucking all that up just because she can't control herself!"

Jamie leaned in closer, wanting to smash the table that kept her body so far from his. "Control is overrated."

She pulled back slightly, moving herself further away. The action caused anger to stir within him and before he knew it he had bared his teeth to her, letting out a low growl.

She raised an eyebrow as she watched him. "What is *wrong* with you?" she asked, folding her arms across her chest. "Seriously, you're acting like you've lost it."

Jamie let an exasperated sigh. "There is *nothing* wrong with me!" he yelled, slamming both of his hands down on the table as he did, the thick white plastic splintering under his fists.

Sam's expression of curiousness quickly turned to one of concern. She placed her hands on either side of his face and moved in closely. For a moment, he thought she was about to kiss him, and was immensely disappointed when she didn't.

"Look in my eyes," she ordered.

Jamie did as he was told, curious as to why she had asked such a thing.

For a few seconds she gazed directly into his eyes, and Jamie held his face just a few inches from hers, breathing in deeply as he inhaled the intoxicating aroma that was Sam.

"Your eyes are bright," she mumbled.

"Do you think they're pretty?" Jamie asked, his tone mocking.

She took her hands from his face and looked at him with an unimpressed expression. "It doesn't look like you're —"

She was cut off by a whooshing sound, Jamie looked up as a flash of blue light appeared beside their table and Danny appeared out of mid-air looking incredibly flustered.

"That's new," Jamie commented.

"Are you insane!" Sam yelled, her eyes wide as she stared at Danny. "You can't portal into the middle of a crowded room."

"I'm shielded," he said, while frantically looking around the room to ensure his claim wasn't unfounded. "Jade is gone," he said. He sounded breathless and Jamie wondered if he'd run around searching for her, or if the use of Magic had drained him.

"Gone?" Jamie looked at him curiously. "What do you me —"

"She's just gone!" he yelled, talking fast. "We went to her house to get some stuff. She went to her room. I felt a Power surge. I heard her scream. By the time I got there she was gone."

"Why would you —"

"*Listen,*" Danny said, cutting Sam off before she could finish. "Earlier on she called me … there was some guy outside the house. I don't know who he is or what he was, but he was apparently looking for Hayley. When I got home he was gone. Apparently Madison vouched for him, so Jade told them both to fuck off and they did. That was just over thirty minutes ago. Coincidence?" He shook his head. "I think not."

"Okay," Sam sighed. She stood and looked in the direction of Scott's table again. Jamie groaned and rolled his eyes. She ignored him. "Madison's not here," she said. "Maybe she's at home. I'll go get her and bring her back to the house, we can deal with her there . . . see what she knows."

Danny shook his head. "They were at our house this morning, that's the first place anyone would look for her," he said, then sent a meaningful glance in Jamie's direction. "We'll need to take her somewhere less populated."

Jamie pointed to himself, dreading the idea of having Sam and Bethany under the same roof. Not that he had any feelings for Bethany, and after the emotional free-falls he'd had with Sam lately, he wasn't sure how he felt about her either.

"You want to take her to my house?"

Danny shrugged. "It would be the best place to keep her," he looked to Sam. "You know Jack would agree."

Sam sighed and looked to Jamie. "Is *she* still there?"

Jamie nodded, and noticed Danny look at him curiously.

"Who's still there?"

"Oh," Sam said with a non-genuine smile. "Jamie's wife . . . forgot to tell you, he's married."

Danny glared at him. "When the fuck did that happen? Have you been cheating with my sister or *on* my sister?" Jamie opened his mouth to speak, but Danny cut him off. "I'm not okay with *either* of them!"

Sam rolled her eyes. "We're not together," she stated. "So technically—"

"Alright!" Jamie yelled in frustration, cutting Sam off before this conversation could continue. "Both of you shut up, you can use my house."

"What about Bethany?" Sam asked, folding her arms across her chest.

Danny glared. "Did he just tell me to shut up?"

"Don't worry about her," Jamie said with a sigh. "She's probably still unconscious."

CHAPTER 18

The girl was unconscious by the time Malachi had carried her through the portal. With a sigh he lowered her to the sofa in the centre of the small cabin he had been using as a hideout since Kraven had been killed.

Slowly, he looked around, briefly missing the room he'd had at the base.

He'd never lived in a home of his own. Since Malachi had been recruited back in the early eighteen-hundreds he had lived at the base with Kraven, first in the training compound, then in the main facility where Kraven stayed.

The man had been kind to him.

He had raised him.

And the Witch had killed him for no good reason.

He closed his eyes and took a breath to calm himself. Anger was pointless; right now he needed to stay calm, if not for the sake of his plan, then for the sake of the human girl he'd just kidnapped.

The girl was the last thing he expected to find on the other side of that portal. Truth be told, he wasn't entirely sure *what* he expected when he'd reopened the portal that Kraven had cast only hours before he died . . . but a girl?

He gazed down at her unconscious form. *Was he planning to recruit her?* Malachi reached out to her with his senses, assessing her soul in every way he could.

A smile spread across his face as he sensed a Power that dwelled within her, buried deep . . . and yet scratching just beneath the surface.

Oh yeah, he thought, *she's got the potential.*

CHAPTER 19

$\mathcal{S}$am opened a portal and transported them to the street outside Madison's house.

Jamie looked around the neighbourhood slowly watching for curious faces peering out from behind curtains; often he'd wondered how people couldn't sense them simply appearing out of nowhere. It made him wonder if—when he'd been human—things like this happened often yet gone unseen by his eyes?

Sam stormed forward, waving her hand in the direction of the house, which caused the door to swing open. She walked inside with no hesitation and Jamie could feel the air crackle around her as tendrils of rage seeped from her every pore. This would be the second time in a week that Jade had been taken and they'd been pointed in Madison's direction. Which as far as Jamie was concerned, was not a good sign and it certainly didn't bode well for the half-Warlock.

Danny followed closely behind Sam as they barged

uninvited into Madison's home, Jamie came in last, showing more hesitation than the other two.

Or perhaps hesitation wasn't correct . . . it wasn't that he feared some disastrous repercussions of their actions, it was more that he wasn't sure what kind of response they expected to get. He was sure that if Madison was part of some kind of nefarious plot she wasn't likely to be forthcoming with information.

A man stormed into the hallway just as Jamie walked through the front door. He was a tall man with red hair, and he glared at them as he moved, seeming completely outraged. "What is the meaning of this!" he demanded with an anger that could easily equal Sam's. Glaring at each of them in turn before his eyes settled back on Sam.

"My friend was kidnapped," Sam began, her voice coming out calm despite the rage that boiled within her. "And your daughter was the last one to see her."

"You are not welcome here," the man stated, taking a confident step in Sam's direction. "You're not one of us, so you're one of *them*. And your *kind* isn't welcome in my home."

Sparks of energy ignited in the palm of Sam's hand, her fingers twitched for a moment before she raised her arm intending to strike the man. Jamie rushed forward, knowing that Sam's energy blast would surely kill him.

He stood between Sam and the man who looked surprised at his intervention. Jamie gazed at him for a moment, then swiftly placed his hand on the man's head and sent a wave of energy into his body, the same way he had with Bethany. The man's legs buckled as he fell into unconsciousness, but Jamie caught him before he hit the floor and carefully lowered him to avoid unnecessary injury.

"Why did you do that!" Sam demanded.

Jamie glared at her, more than annoyed by her attitude and

the tone which she used to address him. "Because you don't *know* if they've done anything wrong. You can't just kill whomever you please."

With a furious sigh, she turned and stormed up the stairs. After spending a moment staring at him in silent confusion Danny followed her. Jamie stayed at the bottom of the stairs, turning his attention to the front door which was still wide open. *She would have killed a man with a possible audience,* he thought, vexed by both her callousness and her carelessness.

Jamie moved forward, slamming the door shut as he ignored the sounds of arguing from upstairs. From what he could hear, Danny seemed to be holding Sam back. With a sigh Jamie followed the sounds of the screaming into a bedroom at the top of the stairs, pushing forward with energy before he even entered the room.

A loud bang and everything was suddenly quiet.

By the time he got there, Madison was unconscious, which he supposed was better than dead.

CHAPTER 20

alachi sat on the wooden table in front of the sofa, staring at the sleeping girl as he wondered how exactly he could explain away the situation.

Mind manipulations were always an option, but psychomanipulation had never been one of his talents. He *could* accomplish it, but not nearly as well as some others could.

With a frown he reached forward hesitantly, momentarily wondering if it would be better to keep her unconscious until he found a way to return her home without being detected. He needed to have a good plan of action before he could risk a fight with Sam . . . She was the most powerful being he'd ever come across, and he didn't hold the Power to defeat her, unless he had a good plan to trap her first.

Killing her wouldn't be impossible . . . just difficult.

Placing his hand on the girl's arm, he shook her. With a gasp she opened her eyes and looked around, seeming panicked. Malachi quickly took his hand away, in case his proximity made the situation worse.

Slowly, she turned her head in his direction, staring at him for a moment, before she jumped to her feet. The sudden movement caused Malachi to fall backwards slightly. "I knew it!" she screamed, pointing an accusing finger in his direction. "I *knew* you were evil!"

"I'm not—"

"Where am I?" she demanded, cutting his words off.

He sighed and rolled his eyes. "What's your name?" he asked, thinking that introductions were always a good place to start.

She simply glared in response. Her green eyes seeming to penetrate his very core; under her gaze he felt like a child being reprimanded by an adult, and instinctively he shrank away from her. *She will do well indeed,* he thought, proud of his find. "I'll ask the questions here!" he declared, attempting to regain some semblance of command.

She turned her gaze in the direction of the door. Malachi followed her line of sight, smiling internally as he wondered if she sensed the wards he'd placed around the perimeter. Without saying another word she stormed towards the door and flung it open. Malachi didn't stop her. He hadn't even counted to five in his head when the air in the living room shimmered and the girl appeared, her eyes wide and stunned as she looked around her. "What the . . . "

She looked in Malachi's direction, and he smiled innocently.

With a glare and a huff, she stormed out the door once more. Repeating the process of an escape attempt despite the fact that it was obviously futile.

He resisted the urge to laugh as she appeared once more, this time looking agitated rather than stunned.

"Open it!" she ordered.

Malachi smiled. "No," he replied. "I have some questions for you. If you answer them you can leave."

She sighed dramatically. "Fine, ask your questions . . . You have ten minutes."

"What's your name?"

"Jade," she replied, then with a large amount of sarcasm added, "You should know that what with you being a pretend member of my mother's coven."

He tried not to smile, instead keeping his expression serious. Which was difficult; serious conversations were not something he had a talent for. "Okay Jade, my name is Malachi—"

"I don't remember asking what *your* name is."

He tried as best as he could to not allow her rudeness to offend him. "Why was there a portal leading to your room?"

"You should know," she said with a glare. "If you opened it then you must be one of *them*."

"Who exactly are *they*?" he asked, wondering if she had already aligned herself with the other side. Or if perhaps she had mistaken him for a Witch.

"You know," she said. "The Warlocks . . . the guys who broke into my room, beat me unconscious, then drowned me."

Malachi stared at her, unable to hide his shock. "Warlocks did *what* to you?"

"Don't pretend you're not one of them!" she yelled. "I'm not an idiot."

"I never claimed you were," he sighed. "Describe the Warlocks."

"Why?" she asked, folding her arms across her chest as she glowered at him.

He rolled his eyes and let a sigh. "Just do it."

"Open the seal and I'll tell you."

"Tell me and I'll open the seal."

"You're holding me prisoner and I'm not okay with it!"

"I'm *not* holding you prisoner . . . I'm just not letting you go before you answer my questions."

Jade let a huff. "Yeah . . . that's, like, the definition of holding someone prisoner, idiot."

"Did you just call me an idiot?" he asked, getting to his feet in an attempt to intimidate her. Slowly, he allowed the glamour that shielded his Powers and make him appear more human to the general population to disappear and allowed her to feel the full weight of his energy as sparks of blue Magic crackled in the air around him.

She stared at him, seeming completely unmoved by his display. Then she folded her arms across her chest. "Am I supposed to be impressed?" she asked rhetorically. "Because I've seen better."

CHAPTER 21

When Jack opened his eyes he found himself to be
staring at a ceiling made of intricately patterned glass
which looked much like an image seen through the lens of a
kaleidoscope, but made entirely of blue shimmering crystal.

With a groan he wondered, *What have the hags done to me
now?* He pushed himself into a sitting position, blinking his
eyes as his vision blurred for a few moments.

With a sigh, he finally turned in their direction, feeling
himself annoyed by the fact that their backs were to him. All
three were sitting cross-legged on the white marble floor, their
bodies forming a circle as they sat with their hands blocking
their eyes. The delicate runes that graced their skin glowed
softly as they chanted.

Jack rolled his eyes as he stood, brushing the dust from his
clothes. For a few moments he simply stood and watched
them, his arms folded across his chest as he grew more and
more irritated by the fact that they continued to ignore his

presence.

Typical, he thought with a sigh.

He took a few steps towards them, pausing on the first step to their alter when he saw images flashing in a circle on the floor between them. Images of Sam . . . and a girl who looked like her, but wasn't.

"What is that?" he asked, his tone serious.

They didn't move as his voice broke the silence of the room, nor did they speak or show any outward reaction. Instead they continued on as though he hadn't said a thing.

With an irate huff, Jack stomped up the thirteen steps to the alter. Not pausing when he reached the top, he shoved his way past them and stood in the centre of their circle, knowing his presence would disturb whatever ritual they were performing.

All three of them sighed in unison, their movements completely mirroring each other as though all three were nothing more than puppets for one single Power. They looked to him, their black soulless eyes causing a chill to course through his blood.

"Hunter," Clotho regarded him with disdain.

"Hag," he shot back, folding his arms as he looked at each of them in turn. "What was that?" he repeated, his eyes settling on Atropos, seer of things to be.

"You disturbed our ritual," Lachesis spoke, staring at her own hands as the symbols stopped glowing.

"What *was* that?" he repeated, knowing he would ask his question as many times as it took for it to be answered.

"The ritual was for Samantha," Atropos spoke, her voice cool and devoid of emotion. "We were making assurances, as is our duty as keepers of prophecy."

For a moment, Jack wondered what would happen with this so called prophecy if they stopped making 'assurances'?

Did their assurances ensure that the prophecy was fulfilled or that it was failed? And why would they interfere at all? As far as he had known, the Moirai were not allowed to interfere, they only prophesised.

Slowly, Jack knelt so that his eyes were level with Atropos. He squinted slightly as he regarded her. "I don't believe that you're supposed to be making *assurances*."

None of them showed any reaction to his statement. Instead, Atropos replied, "We will complete our task without question of why it is to be, only knowing that it must be. And you, *Hunter*, you will complete your task as you must, and you would do well to refrain from asking so many questions."

CHAPTER 22

$\mathcal{J}$amie stood with his back to the front door as he sipped the blood from his flask, watching Sam secure Madison to a chair with a slight sense of amusement. She stood with a sigh, looking at him over her shoulder momentarily. "Wake her up," she ordered.

Without moving an inch, Jamie lifted the shield of Power he'd placed on her mind to keep her placid and unconscious. Madison's eyes instantly shot open, and frantically she looked around the room. "Where am I?"

Sam leaned on the back of the sofa as she watched Madison. "Where's Jade?" she asked, ignoring Madison's question.

"Jade? Wha—" Madison snapped her mouth shut, pausing as she seemed to take a moment to think. "I don't know."

"Liar," Sam said calmly. "Jade told Danny you were in my backyard about an hour ago. She said you vouched for some guy . . . I didn't get a description, but if I had to guess I'd say he was your boyfriend."

"I don't have a—"

"Sorry," Sam said with a smile. "Your boss. Michael, was it?"

Madison huffed. "His name isn't—"

"Sorry," she said again. "I'm not good with names, especially when they don't matter. What does matter is where he is, and why he took Jade. And more importantly, has he hurt her?"

"He wouldn't hurt her," Madison whispered, though she sounded slightly uncertain.

"Well," said Sam. "I'm glad you have so much faith in him, because everything he does to Jade, I'm going to do to you."

"Sam—" Danny tried to interrupt, probably to talk some sense into her, but she continued as though he hadn't spoken.

"*Or,*" she began, bending forward so that she was at eye level with Madison, "you could do yourself a favour and tell me where he is, if she's not there I'll leave you in peace."

Madison stared up at Sam, her face a mask of disbelief. Jamie saw that behind her back she was moving her hands, testing the restraints that kept her bound. He smiled slightly, knowing that there was no chance of her gaining her freedom that way. Surely she knew that her only hope was to cooperate with Sam.

After a moment, she seemed to realise that the ropes were not going to break, and she sighed, her shoulders dropping in defeat. "Sam . . . this is ridiculous. You have to know that right? Why can't you see that we're on the same side!"

Sam scowled, her lips set in a harsh line as she stared down at Madison. "You betrayed me. You, and your kind, you're always trying to kill me . . . so, how can you—"

"We're not trying to fucking kill you! Our side has *never* tried to kill you. We've all gone out of our way to make sure you weren't harmed. We don't want you dead, we want you on our side. Like it or not, this is your world too . . . It's your responsibility to help defend it, just as much as it is anyone else's."

"This was *never* my war! I never wanted any part of this, and I've told you all that countless times! I said I just wanted to be left alone! I said that me and my friends are off limits!"

Madison's eyes began to well up with tears, and Jamie almost felt sorry for her. "But, I am your friend Sam. I'm your friend, and I need your help."

Sam took a step back and stared at Madison for a moment, her expression seeming both surprised and upset over the other girl's words.

"Sam," Danny began, placing a hand on her shoulder. "Maybe we should —"

"No," Sam interrupted, her voice shaking. "You *were* my friend, but then you chose to become one of them."

Jamie watched in silence as Sam turned her back to him, and stormed up the stairs. It wasn't until he saw the reflection of the light on silver when she emerged from his bedroom and stomped back down, that he realised what she had gone up for.

She stalked over the Madison and held a dagger to her throat.

"Sam!" Danny yelled, his voice alarmed.

Jamie simply observed, feeling slightly amused by the scene unfolding before him, knowing that Sam had no intention of actually using the weapon she brandished. If Sam *did* intend to hurt Madison, and if her emotions were so out of control that she felt the need to kill her former friend, Jamie knew that she would have used her Magic, as she always had.

"Shut up," Sam said calmly, directing her words at Danny who did nothing but glare at the back of her head. "Tell me where he has her, or I swear to the Gods, I *will* kill you. And I will do it slowly."

Madison's eyes widened as she stared fearfully at the blade that was pointed to her throat.

"You have five seconds," Sam said, before she began counting. "Five."

"You've got it all wrong!" Madison said.

"Four."

"Sam, I can't—"

"*Three.*"

"Just listen to me!"

"*Two.*"

"Stop!" Madison screamed. "I was at your house to stop him!"

Sam lowered the knife slightly. "Go on."

Madison let a sigh, which sounded half relieved, half irritated. "You killed Kraven, and he wants revenge. But he's just upset, he'll calm down soon. I swear to you if he took Jade he wouldn't hurt her. I *swear.*"

Sam clenched her jaw, it was obvious to Jamie that her patience was beginning to run out. "Where can I find him?"

"There's a cabin, just outside of town." She nodded in the direction of the door. "That way, through the woods in the direction opposite to where we are now."

Jamie squinted his eyes, his head tilted slightly as he thought back, her description triggering memories from the previous months. "I know that place," he said. All three people in the room turned to look at him. "I've been there before."

"You were the one who killed those people?" Madison asked, her voice a whisper.

Jamie did nothing but shrug in response.

Sam let a sigh. "Alright, you lead the way," she said to Jamie, before turning to Madison. "You better hope he hasn't hurt her."

"Let me come with you," Madison begged, her cheeks stained black by her running mascara. "I can help. Just listen—"

"No," Sam snapped as she snatched her coat from the back of the sofa, letting the dagger fall from her hands and to the cushions below. "I'm sick of trying to be recruited by you and your people, so you can spend the time I'm gone thinking about something."

"Sam, I—"

"The Witches want me dead," Sam interrupted, "the Demons, meaning you and your people, want me dead . . . so as far as I'm concerned there are, not two, but three sides to this battle. The Witches, the Demons, and me. I suggest you take the time to choose your side wisely."

CHAPTER 23

*J*ade stood across from Malachi, her arms folded across her chest her as they had a staring contest. She watched him, daring him with her eyes to strike out at her, and though he stood tensely as though he was about to, he hadn't yet.

Which was why she was confident he wasn't going to attack her.

After a few moments of glaring at each other, Jade let a tired sigh, and glanced towards the door before looking back to him, the Warlock who was now holding her hostage, though he had yet to admit that aloud. "Are you done making yourself look stupid yet?"

He glared. "You'd do well not to insult me."

She rolled her eyes, unmoved by his empty threats. "Whatever, like I said, not impressed. If you're going to kill me, kill me . . . if you're not going to kill me, then open the seal."

Malachi watched her for a moment longer, then slowly his appearance began to shift.

There weren't any noticeable differences in how he made himself look physically, in fact there were no changes in his physical appearance at all, the change was something indescribable that just made him *feel* more normal. Jade took a deep breath, not realising how heavy the air had become until it had been restored.

For a while they stood opposite each other, glaring. Jade's heart was pounding so loudly she felt it reverberate through her ears. She was sweating and in all honesty felt as though she was about to throw up. This was the second time in the past few days that a Warlock had pulled her through a portal, and brought her to this same place. The last time it hadn't ended well for her, and although she was afraid right now, she wasn't going to give this man the satisfaction of seeing her express her fear. So she stood straight and stared him directly in the eyes, and feigning boredom said, "Your ten minutes are up. Now open it."

He spent a few more seconds watching her, his gaze uncomfortably assessing. But then, he tilted his head to the side and smiled, though he didn't seem amused. "You haven't answered my questions yet."

"Yeah, well you wasted your question time by acting like a moron, so that's your fault. Now open it."

He shoved his hands into the pockets of his jeans and rolled back on his heels. "No," he said simply.

"We had a deal!" she yelled, taking a small step away from him.

"I said I would open the seal when you had answered some questions for me. You haven't answered my questions."

Jade let an exasperated sigh. "I am so sick of being kidnapped," she mumbled.

"I haven't kidnapped you," Malachi said, his tone defensive.

For a moment she glared at him in disbelief, thinking that he should really read a dictionary, or Google the definition of the word 'kidnapped'.

He rolled his eyes and let a sigh. "Just describe the Warlocks, that's all the information I want from you, then you have my word I will take you home."

Jade watched him for a few seconds as she attempted to gauge whether he was being sincere. It was difficult to decipher his level of honesty, but if he claimed a description was all he wanted, there was no reason for her *not* to tell him. "I'm not sure," she said, watching his expression for any hint of a reaction. "I was reading when a portal opened in my room. I was knocked over the head, so I didn't get a good look. Everyone told me one of them was killed though, they said his body is in the ocean."

Malachi's expression seemed to remain neutral, although she could tell by the slight quiver in his lips that he was trying very hard to keep it that way. He opened his mouth, as though he was about to respond, when his words were cut off by the sound of the door being thrown open.

She turned swiftly towards it, curious as to how someone could barge in when the place was locked. She found herself even more surprised when she recognised the man who stormed into the room. "Mr Parker?" Jade looked at him in confusion, though he barely seemed to care about the fact that she was there. He didn't take more than a second to regard her, before he turned his glaring eyes in the direction of her captor.

"What is it Lucas?" Malachi asked, his tone tinged with irritation.

Mr Parker glared for a moment, his jaw clenching as though

he was trying to suppress a great amount of rage. "So you *did* take her," he said. Malachi opened his mouth to speak, but Mr Parker continued. "Because of *you*, my house was broken into by *her* . . . again. And she took my daughter. Because for some inconceivable reason, she protected you this morning. And now they have her."

Malachi seemed genuinely surprised. "Sam took Madison?"

Jade stared at Mr Parker as she allowed his words to sink in. *Sam kidnapped Madison . . . typical.* She sighed and looked from Mr Parker to Malachi and back again. She could tell by the look in Mr Parker's eyes that he was on the verge of violence, and she was sure that by the way he was glaring at Malachi that not all of it was directed at Sam.

Though by Malachi's thoughtful expression and calculating smile it was obvious that he either didn't see Mr Parker as a threat, despite the fact that the man was bigger and older than him — at least Jade thought he was older — or he was simply oblivious to the beating obviously coming his way.

Malachi's gaze slowly shifted in her direction, and he smiled slowly. "*Now* I'm kidnapping you."

CHAPTER 24

$\mathcal{I}$t took them almost two hours to travel from one end of the woods to the other. Sam had suggested that they portal the whole way there, but both Jamie and Danny agreed that it would have been a bad idea. Since Jamie was the only one, besides Madison, who actually knew where they were going, there wasn't a good chance that Sam would be able to portal them directly to their destination, and if they didn't make it there in one go they risked Sam's Power being sensed by anyone who may have been inside at the time.

As a compromise they had portaled half way through the woods in order to minimise the amount of time they would have to spend on foot. Which meant the journey took them two hours instead of however long it would have taken them without the portal.

Jamie walked in front with Danny and Sam trailing along behind him. They came to a clearing within the trees, beyond which was the cabin from Jamie's memories. He paused, turning to Sam for an indication of what they were to do next.

When he looked at her he saw that she was glaring at the cabin, as though the building itself was the enemy. He noticed how the muscle in her jaw clenched as she stared, and as he gazed downwards he saw that her hands had formed fists so tight her knuckles were turning white.

He turned his gaze in Danny's direction. He was also watching Sam, his expression one of concern. Turning away from them both, Jamie faced the cabin and took a deep breath to calm himself, reaching outwards with his senses.

It didn't take long for him to gauge who was and wasn't in the building, mainly because when he reached out he found it to be empty. His shoulders relaxed slightly. "No one's home," he stated.

Sam didn't look at him, and her body didn't seem to relax at his words. "She was here," was all she said, before she began moving forward.

Danny was quick to follow, reaching out to her as if to hold her back. But she moved too quickly and his hand missed her. "It could be trapped!" he yelled after her as she stormed up to the door.

Jamie followed her at a more casual pace as he psychically reached out once more, wondering if there was some psychic indication that would have led Sam to believe that Jade had been here, or if it was just her wishful thinking.

There was a crash from in front of him, and he didn't need to look to know that Sam had kicked the door down.

He followed her and Danny inside.

"No one's home," said Danny with a sigh. "Just like he said. Maybe we can—"

"*No*," Sam snapped, turning when she had reached the centre of what appeared to be the living room. "She *was* here."

"I can't get a sense of that," Jamie mumbled, running his

hand through his hair as he looked around. Noticing that there was no sign of the damage he'd caused the last time he'd been here.

Sam grumbled irritably. "I *know* she was here, it's just a feeling I have, okay? Stop questioning me and help me find something that will tell me where they took her."

Jamie let a sigh as he looked around the room. "I don't mean to point out the obvious, but if they moved her it's because they knew we were coming. So they probably moved her somewhere else. Somewhere we can't find as easily."

"Or somewhere they *want* us to find easily," Danny said with a glance in his direction. "If I was them, and I wanted to kill Sam who was coming to kill me because I took her friend, I'd take that friend somewhere I'd have the advantage, and the time to set a trap that would ensure I win, if there was a fight."

"You think they're using Jade as bait?" Sam asked incredulously.

Danny shrugged. "It's what I'd do. I mean, they already took her, might as well use her while they can."

"So where would they take her?" Jamie asked.

"Main base," Sam replied, as she pushed past him and Danny towards the front door. "That's the only place they could take her where I couldn't follow."

Jamie sighed as he turned to follow her outside. "So now we just need to go to their main base. What are the odds of *that* ending well?"

"The odds aren't good," Danny replied. "But I've yet to witness a plan of Sam's where the odds *are* in our favour."

CHAPTER 25

When Jack opened his eyes he was standing in the living room of Sam's house. He blinked for a moment, slightly disorientated from the sudden change of scenery. No matter how many times he was transported between places the seamlessness that occurred between one place and the other always left him feeling out of sorts.

With a sigh he looked around, searching for whoever was home.

He was surprised to find the house empty as he'd thought that he would find at least Jade and Danny inside.

So he teleported himself to the high school, making sure to stay in a non-corporeal and invisible form so that no one would notice his arrival. When he got there classes were in session, and from what he recalled Sam should have been in history at this time.

She wasn't.

And when he paused to scan the school for any presence of

anything non-human, he found that neither Sam nor Jamie were even in the building.

With another sigh, he decided to teleport himself to the only other place he could think to look.

Jamie's house.

When he got there however, he was extremely surprised to not only find that the house was empty of Sam, Jamie, Jade and Danny, but the only person in the house that he could find was Madison.

And she was tied to a chair.

She jumped slightly as he appeared in front of her, and stared at him wide eyed and afraid.

"What . . . the fuck . . . is going on?" he asked slowly.

Madison's bottom lip quivered slightly, and then she began to cry.

CHAPTER 26

When they arrived back at Jamie's home, deciding this time that they would use a portal to travel the entire journey, they found Jack was already there, and he was releasing Madison from her bindings as tears streamed from her eyes.

Jack looked up angrily as they entered the house. Jamie found himself slightly annoyed by the fact that he was being glared at as he entered his own home. But he said nothing. Instead he walked into his house and stood by the door with his arms folded across his chest.

"Why are you letting her out?" Sam demanded as she walked over to Jack.

He stood — Madison now free — and glared down at Sam.

Jamie stood straighter as he watched Jack standing taller than Sam with interest.

Somewhere in the back of his mind he had thought of Sam as one of the most imposing creatures he'd ever met in his life.

But watching her now, she seemed small in comparison to Jack, who was larger than her in both height and muscle mass.

"I leave you alone for half a day and you decide to spend it kidnapping half-Warlocks and tying them up in Jamie's house? Either you've lost your mind, or you've started a BDSM club. Which one is it?"

Sam's jaw twitched. "You don't know what happened!"

"Yes I do!" Jack yelled. "Madison told me everything before you got here. I did *not* raise you to be like this Sam, you need to stop it. Learn to be calm and do things rationally. You don't need more enemies than you already have. What you did last week, I will *not* put up with again."

"But they—"

"No!" he interrupted her. Jamie glanced sideways at Danny who seemed to be taking an unusual interest in the contents of the bookshelf, his expression uncomfortable as he stared. "We will do this properly."

Sam threw her hands up in the air and scoffed, before she turned her back to Jack and folded her arms across her chest, sulking.

Jack sighed tiredly and turned to face Madison. "Obviously Jade wasn't there, so I think Sam owes you an—"

"Jade was there," Sam mumbled. Jack turned to face her slowly. Sam didn't move. "Or at least she *had* been. Who knows where she is now, or what they're doing to her."

Jack frowned and turned to Madison.

The frightened girl looked to Sam in horror, then back to Jack. "I didn't think he actually took her," she said. "But I wanna help get her back."

Sam scoffed and rolled her eyes.

Danny sighed. "We think she may have been taken to the main base, but obviously, we don't know how to get there. You could draw us a map, and then you can go home."

"What?" Sam looked to him in utter disbelief. "Go home? Where she can call them and —"

"I'll take you there myself," Madison said, holding her head high as if to prove that Sam was wrong about her, as if the accusations didn't affect her in the slightest when Jamie could tell that she was hurt. "There's a portal at home that leads straight there. I'll get us through it, then I'll help you find Jade. If he did take her, he'll probably have her in one of the cells. There's a lot of tunnels though, you might get lost if you go alone."

Jack nodded. "Alright," he said, glancing at Sam one last time. "Lead the way."

CHAPTER 27

After Malachi locked the girl in the dungeon he set about preparing his plan very quickly. Lucas followed him the whole time, but he pretended that he couldn't see the man glaring at him with all the hatred he had within his body.

Malachi was almost certain that Madison wouldn't be harmed, and all they had to do once he'd succeeded in taking Sam out of the equation was locate her. Which should be simple due to the fact that Sam didn't have many resources, and therefore didn't have access to all that many places to hide a person.

He was confident that they would be able to find Madison before the end of the day.

"If she's so much as scratched," Lucas said as Malachi put the final touches on his trap. "I *will* kill you."

Malachi looked at him over his shoulder and nodded, confused as to how Lucas could think that he didn't care for

Madison just as much as he did. "If anything happens to her, I will gladly accept my death."

And then, they waited.

CHAPTER 28

$\mathcal{B}$ethany listened, unmoving from the bed Jamie had left her lying on this morning.

There were people downstairs.

She was waiting for them to leave.

Three hours she stayed in perfect stillness doing nothing but listening for the house to empty. And when the moment finally came that everyone had left, she waited some more. Just in case anyone happened to come back inside while she was up.

When she was sure the coast was clear, she pushed herself off the mattress, slightly annoyed by the fact that Jamie — who was less than a week older than her in Vampire terms, and four years younger than her in human ones — had greater abilities than she did.

Even with her extensive knowledge on the subject of Vampires, she didn't have the Power to influence the mind of non-humans, especially not others of her species. Yet somehow *he* had managed it. A mere child compared to her.

And when did he stop being so nice? she thought with a huff.

She only had vague memories of Jamie, since she had known him so long ago and had been so busy since then, but from what she did remember the boy was a hopeless romantic, as honest as the day was long and polite beyond all reason. Yet once he'd overcome his shock at the first sight of her, alive and well, he'd glared at her and demanded to know what she wanted. As if she had come to extort something from him ... as though that was something he expected of her. He'd given her use of his bed, and not slept beside her, but not because he was being polite ... because he wasn't using his bed at the time. And he'd used his Power to knock her unconscious on more than one occasion.

Never mind the fact that he had outright told her to get out of his home.

The reason she had chosen to bother finding him at all was because she knew what a sap he was when it came to damsels in distress. If she had known he would be so uncooperative she would have found a way to Aleczander herself and come back to kill him later.

Oh well, she thought as she stood, slowly making her way down the stairs. It wasn't as though she'd ever really cared for him, so she hadn't suffered much of a loss.

She made her way down the stairs slowly, looking around as she entered the living room. In the space between the sofa and the front door was a chair that appeared to be part of a dining set, which was confusing because as far as she had seen, there was no kitchen furniture in his home.

With a shake of her head, and ignoring the bindings that were lying on the floor around the chair, she ventured into the living room. Keeping her eyes open for anything interesting.

Bethany smiled when her eyes settled on the small object

that was resting on the coffee table.

His phone.

She ran over and grabbed it. Going to the contacts where she hoped to find something useful.

With a smile, she clicked on Aleczander's number and sent him a message asking if they could meet somewhere as soon as he was available, mildly irritated by the fact that the only other contact he had was that girl.

But that was inconsequential now.

They would all be dead quite soon . . .

CHAPTER 29

True to her word, Madison led them safely through the portal. When they got to the other side, the room — if you could call it a room — was vacant of other beings.

Jack was the last one through, and Jamie peered over his shoulder as the swirl of light vanished into nothingness. With a sigh, he looked around.

The air was musty, cold and slightly damp. "Where are we?" he asked.

"Underground," Madison replied. "Geographically, we're everywhere. Everywhere there's land, there's tunnels."

He looked down a tunnel that was lit by orange and yellow light that seemed to be coming from within the walls themselves.

"Which way?" Danny asked.

"This whole level is the dungeon. Down that way," she pointed straight ahead, "it splits, then splits again. There's a *lot* of them."

"So we each take one," said Jack. "Walk to the end, check the cells. If it veers off, we turn back. Meet here. Regroup. Take a new tunnel."

Jamie looked to Sam when he heard her mumble profanities under her breath. When he compared the expression on her face to the expression on everyone else's it was clear that she was the *only* one who had an issue with Jack's plan.

Everyone walked forward dutifully while Sam stood where she was, her arms folded across her chest.

"What exactly is your problem *now*?" Jamie asked, his question coming out in a more hostile way than he'd intended. Looking forward, he saw the others walk on, as though they hadn't noticed that neither he nor Sam had followed.

Sam glared at him. "What's *my* problem?" she asked, though it was obvious that the question was rhetorical.

"Yes," he replied. "What's your problem?" He glared at her as she was him, when he saw the fury in her eyes something clicked within his brain. He smiled slowly and leaned in closer to avoid being overheard, not that it would have been an issue given the fact that everyone was well out of earshot. "Are you angry that you don't get to kill her?"

She slapped him.

Hard.

Jamie reeled back, placing a hand to his cheek, blinking his eyes as he tried to regain his senses. "What's *your* problem?" she asked, taking a step towards him. "There is something *seriously wrong* with you lately."

He felt her fury fill the air around her.

He breathed in her aura; her aggression felt intoxicating, and contagious.

He smiled once more, this time innocently. "There's nothing wrong with me," he said, taking his hand away from his face. "And there's no need for violence, we were just having a conversation. After all, bloodlust is something we have in common, isn't it?"

She scoffed, shook her head and walked away from him.

Jamie followed her down the tunnel. They both paused when they came to where it veered off into four sections. Pushing out with his senses he could tell that the first three were occupied by Madison, Danny and Jack. He turned towards the last one, directing forward with his arm. "Shall I go first, or do you want the honour?"

Sam rolled her eyes and barged ahead.

"I'm not kidding Jamie," she said as they walked. "There's something wrong with you, you've been acting like a crazy person all week."

"You can't know that for a fact," he stated. "I was ignoring you at the start of the week."

"You know—"

"*Perhaps*," he interrupted her, "I'm still angry with you. After all you did kill a man who had been possessed, implying that all people who ever hurt you . . . even while not in control of their actions, deserve to be killed."

"I didn't mean you," she said quietly. "I don't blame you for that."

He smiled slowly. "I said perhaps . . . it's not definite. I *could* be angry about that, or I could just be annoyed by you in general." He shrugged. "I'm not sure exactly which one. Perhaps it's both . . . perhaps it's neither. Either way, you've made it clear that you don't care about feelings, so it's not your business, so don't imply there's something wrong with *me* when *you're* the one pretending you're better than you are."

She gawked at him for a moment, then asked, "Do you *want* me to hit you again?"

"Do you want to answer my question?"

They stopped walking when the tunnel split into three more sections. Sam turned to face him. "What question?"

"Are you angry that you don't get to kill Madison?"

With no warning, she reached forward swiftly, scratching once at his cheek.

Jamie moved away from her quickly, glaring at her for a moment before he saw the expression on her face as she stared at his blood on her nails and he realised that she had only hurt him to draw blood.

With a fascination bordering on infatuation, he watched as she brought her crimson stained nails to her lips and licked the blood from them.

His lips curved in a smile as he allowed his wounds to heal, rubbing his cheek to ensure that there were no scars. "If you wanted a taste, all you had to do was ask."

Then he kissed her. Grabbing hold and pulling her close.

Biting his tongue, letting blood flow from it before he parted his lips, and hers.

He had expected it to last longer than it did, as when they kissed before it lasted for quite a while and usually led to other things. But barely a second after his tongue touched hers she shoved him away, breaking their contact.

Which made him angry beyond all reason.

Allowing his cuts to heal, and wiping the blood from his lips, he took a step in her direction and yelled, "You were the one who started it!" She didn't back away. "You tasted my blood!"

"Yeah," she said with a glare. "That does *not* mean I want more of it!"

He sighed irritably and folded his arms across his chest. "You kiss me whenever you want to."

"So?"

"Oh, so you can use me, but I can't use you? I won't lie . . . this relationship feels rather one sided."

Sam scoffed and rolled her eyes. "I was just making sure you were still you and not a Shifter in disguise. But it turns out you're not a Shifter, you're just an asshole." She pointed to the first tunnel. "You take that one."

Without another word, she turned and stormed away.

CHAPTER 30

*J*ade wasn't sure exactly where she was. The guy who *'hadn't'* kidnapped her had pulled her through another portal and dropped her off in what she was almost sure was some kind of prison.

For a while she had just banged on the heavy metal door, yelling at him or anyone else who may have been outside to let her out. No one responded and after a while her hand became so sore from all the banging that she had given up, instead taking a moment to catch her breath and get her bearings. Taking the time to take a good look around where she was, attempting to see if there was perhaps another way out.

The room she was in was small. The walls were made of what appeared to be cobblestone, and the floor was merely trampled dirt. There were no windows, yet the room was bright. From what she could tell the light was emanating from some symbols carved high up on the walls. And no matter how long she stared at them, she couldn't make sense of what they were. Although she guessed, from the effect they had that they were some kind of magical symbol which was used in lieu of an electric light.

The cell was empty of *anything*. Within it was no furniture; not a chair for sitting on while awaiting interrogation, and not one of those crappy metal framed beds you'd expect to see inside a cell. The whole room had the appearance and the feel of a place where you would leave a person you wanted to forget about, someone you wanted to simply waste away and die quietly.

Which was something that Jade, a nineteen year old girl with an infinite number of plans for a life which began at college next September and ended in a death caused by old age, was not prepared to accept.

Though after over two hours of standing in her dank cell, she felt there was nothing that she could do to get herself out.

The door was too heavy for her to attempt to break.

There was nothing around her, or that she had on her, that could perhaps be used to pick the lock.

There were no windows for her to climb out of.

No escape route that she could see.

With a tired sigh she let herself sink to the ground. Not caring about the dirt that would stain her jeans, or how many people had inhabited this cell before her and had probably bled to death on the floor.

She just sat, and instead thought of the people she knew outside of the cell who would surely be searching for her. And wondered, knowing that she was nothing more than bait, if she really wanted to be found.

CHAPTER 31

$\mathcal{S}$am marched down the hallway, too preoccupied with her annoyance to pay attention to her surroundings and by the time she'd managed to calm herself she had no idea where she was.

The place she was standing now looked nothing like the tunnel she had walked down with Jamie. The stone walls were now bricks of concrete, more modern in appearance than the older looking tunnel they'd arrived in. She paused and looked behind her, all that she could see was modern looking walls and floors, which meant that she must have taken a wrong turn somewhere.

Did I take any *turns?* she thought in confusion, not having any recollection of how she came to be here.

She looked to either side. There were no doors, which meant that there was no way Jade could be in this area.

Deciding that there was something about where she was that didn't feel quite right, she turned, walking back the way she came.

Each part of the tunnel she walked past looked exactly the same as the parts before. No matter how much she walked, she never seemed to actually move, always ending up where she started.

After five minutes of walking and getting nowhere Sam froze, suddenly feeling as though something was really wrong.

If nothing else she should have walked by at least one door by now, or at the very least be able to see one up ahead. She took a breath and listened, trying to gain sense of something or someone. The area was eerily quiet, and as she stretched her senses she felt nothing reciprocate, which meant that either there was absolutely no one within range, or that everyone who was nearby was keeping themselves shielded from her.

With a reluctant sigh, and an irate groan, she focused her energy on the one aura she had come to know quite well, and was thus able to connect with from even miles away.

<Jamie!> she yelled psychically, projecting louder than necessary, knowing that the volume would give him a slight headache, as he'd annoyed her to the point that she wanted to hurt him in some way.

There was a moment of silence in which she knew he had heard her and was ignoring her on purpose.

She sighed once more. <Don't be a dick and answer me>

<I don't appreciate the name calling, or the yelling, or the constant rejections, so tell me, what exactly do I get for participation in this conversation?>

Sam rolled her eyes as she walked forward, using the psychic link with Jamie as a compass to lead her to where she knew there was other people. <How about I don't murder you?>

A moment in which she was almost sure she could sense his

mocking laughter, followed by silence as he didn't bother responding.

Sam stopped walking, pushing her senses out further, hoping that she could perhaps make contact with someone more helpful, like Jack. But she could sense nothing from the others. Even Jamie's mind seemed further away than it should have been.

The tunnel he was in ran parallel to the one she was stuck inside of, so he should have felt close, yet his mind barely registered as a blip on the very edge of her senses. If it wasn't for the fact that she knew his mind as well as she did, she was sure that she wouldn't have been able to sense him either.

A knot began to form in the pit of her stomach, her heart pounding loudly as she was suddenly struck by the realisation that she was further away from the others than she should have been. Almost as though she'd been deliberately separated.

She clenched her jaw as she turned swiftly in every direction, checking every area she could for signs of Magic. It was then that she sensed the distinct aura of a dimensional bubble, the seams of which were made invisible by countless runes which glowed as she began to focus her senses on them.

Sam ran at full speed, despite knowing as she did that it wouldn't matter, due to the lock on the dimension she was trapped. Even so she ran, hoping that her constant movement would make it difficult for anyone to catch her.

As she reached the end of the dimension she would simply pass through a veil that would continue the loop and place her back at the beginning where she knew, if not now then soon enough, someone would be waiting for her.

Once more she reached out to Jamie, hoping that he would care enough to help her despite the fact that she could feel a strange taint on his soul every time she reached towards him.

<I don't care if you're pissed, I need your help> she began, running through the veil at the end of the dimension, appearing back where she started.

No one was there.

She kept running.

<I walked into a trap>

A stirring as she finally felt him respond. *<What do you – >*

<Shut up and listen> she interrupted. *<I walked into a trap. I don't know where I am right now, but I'm not in the tunnel anymore. They'll be here soon enough. Do me a favour and punch Madison for me>*

<Stay still> he said. *<I'm coming to you>*

<No point. You can't find me>

<Is that a challenge?>

Sam laughed despite herself, the sound coming out with difficulty as her lungs struggled to deal with the breathlessness from running and laughing at the same time. *<Don't be an idiot>*

She continued running forward, sensing the end of the loop up ahead. She ran through it, coming out at the beginning, where this time there were people waiting for her. Before she had a chance to use any of her Powers, someone shot her with a tranquiliser gun.

The dart hit her neck, and weakened her instantly.

Several hands caught her before she hit the ground.

Before the darkness overtook her she heard a push in the back of her head, a voice which said, *<Challenge accepted>*

CHAPTER 32

Danny wandered through the tunnels in a straight line as Madison had instructed, his instincts on edge the entire time as he waited to walk into the inevitable trap.

Apart from the cell doors which lined the walls, there were no crevices for anyone—or anything—to be hiding in. Not that the 'Demons', as they called themselves, really needed crevices for hiding. If they wished it he was sure they could simply spell their way through the walls.

The cells he had checked so far had been empty. Apparently the Demons had way more cells than prisoners, which generally wasn't a good sign as it meant that they either no longer used this area he had wasted countless moments wandering, or that they simply killed whomever they took.

With a sinking feeling in the pit of his stomach, he continued moving, his sights set on the door ahead which appeared to be the last one before the tunnel split once more.

He came to the door, which was made of a heavy steel like all the ones before, and reached his hand to it. The metal was cold to the touch and, as he heaved the door open just enough to peer inside, he found the cell to be just as empty as all the ones before.

With a sigh and a distraught glance around the seemingly endless string of tunnels, he decided to turn back. Knowing that everyone else would be doing the same if they hadn't already.

Once he got back he would suggest that they try a different method of searching, as so far the aimless wandering had proven fruitless.

For him at least.

Not two steps after he began making his way back to the portal, he froze, sure that he'd heard something coming from behind.

Slowly, Danny looked over his shoulder and towards the area where the tunnel split in two.

For a moment, he simply stood, his fists clenching tightly by his sides as his mind aggressively began to bombard him with images of all the things that could be making their way towards him.

Deciding that he wouldn't back away from a fight, no matter how outgunned he may be, he turned on his heel and marched directly towards the sound with purpose.

Once in the main tunnel's offshoot he glared at the space ahead, unable to see anything coming towards him. The tunnel he stood in now was just as empty as the one before.

Danny stopped moving, his head turned to the side, eyes squinted in concentration as he listened. Focusing all of his energy on amplifying his ability to hear any and all noises in the vicinity.

He heard it again.

The scraping of metal on metal.

Turning sharply, he ran towards the source of the sound, stopping when he came face to face with another metal door. He slapped his hand against it, hard, and yelled, "Jade! Are you in there?"

"Who is it?" a voice replied from the other side of the door.

Danny felt himself awash with relief when he recognised the voice as Jade's. He laughed slightly. "Who do you think it is?" he asked sarcastically.

"I dunno," she said. Inside the sound of scraping continued. "But you better get me the fuck outta here, and if Sam's around, tell her to go home."

"What are you doing in there?" he asked curiously, wondering what the scraping noise was as he hunkered down, feeling at the edges of the door for any parts that felt less sturdy than the rest.

"Trying to scratch out the marks on the door," she replied. "I think they might be what's keeping it locked."

Danny straightened and placed his hand on the door.

The metal was warm where it should have been cold, and when he closed his eyes and gently pushed at it with his senses he could feel the soft hum of Magic ingrained into the very metal of the door, keeping it sealed.

But though he could sense Magic on it, he was unable to tell if the spell was to keep the door sealed or if it also had an alarm system which would activate once any of the other runes had been broken.

"I'm going to break the door open," he said with a resolute sigh. "You might want to step back, and I sure as hell hope you're ready to run once it's open."

"Why would I need to run?" Jade asked, her voice growing more distant as she moved away from the door.

"In case anyone feels it," he replied.

With a deep breath, not taking his hand off the door, Danny sent out a blast of energy, targeting the very Magic that was holding it in place. A flash of blue surrounded the door, fading slowly as it worked its way through, causing the runes to glow softly before one by one they disappeared.

It didn't feel as though any alarms had been triggered, but even so he moved swiftly, tearing the door open and grabbing Jade by the arm, pulling her behind him as he ran.

It wasn't until they reached the end of the tunnel that the guards arrived.

CHAPTER 33

*J*amie ran through the tunnel that Sam had been walking down, knowing as he entered it that she wouldn't be there.

She had disconnected their thoughts only seconds ago, and he had all but lost sense of her. By the time he got to a junction at the end of the tunnel, he knew that he needed to look elsewhere. Pausing for a moment, he closed his eyes and focused. If this had all been a trap to capture Sam, then the odds were that she would be wherever the people who owned this maze were. With a deep breath to calm his racing thoughts he pushed his senses outwards, probing every crevice and shadow in every tunnel and every room.

Jack was the closest presence he could feel, and as his senses stretched further he could feel the mind of Madison, then Danny, who appeared to have located Jade. He continued to push. All the areas on his level appeared to be vacant of anyone. It wasn't until he began to reach upwards that he gained a sense of those who lived in this so called base.

He latched onto the first mind he could find and forced his way inside.

From that mind he first searched for an image of Sam, of which he found none. With a sigh he continued his hunt, pulling every image, memory and thought of the area in which the 'Demons' lived.

His eyes opened once he had a clear sense of direction, and he ran through the tunnels until he found a door made of wood, knowing now that wooden doors marked the exits just as metal doors marked the cells.

As Jamie ran he sent out small bursts of energy every few steps, hoping that one of these bursts would pick up Sam's aura, allowing him to sense her.

At the end of that tunnel, and a few turns later, there was a wooden door. Jamie ran to it without slowing his pace or stopping to allow himself time to properly open the door. Instead running at it at high speed, jaw clenched as he braced for impact.

The door burst with a loud—and highly audible to everyone in the vicinity—bang. Covered in wooden splinters and paying no mind to the men who appeared from nowhere to hold him back, he continued running, moving up the staircase.

In his current location he could vaguely sense Sam, knowing by the lack of resistance in her mind that she was unconscious.

He pushed through the group of men who all tried to grab onto him in an attempt to restrain him. Not stopping to kill them as instinct seemed to demand he should, knowing that if he wasted any time with them he would not get to Sam before it was already too late.

Once he reached the upper level, beyond the staircase, he found a hallway filled with more people who all turned to stare as he ran past, though he knew that at the speed he was moving there wasn't a single one of them who could see him clearly.

He could feel Sam clearer now, and using his senses to guide him, he navigated the halls until he came to a heavily guarded room.

Grinding his teeth in annoyance as the six guards all raised weapons or glowing hands in his direction. Something in the back of his mind seemed to snap beneath the weight of his anger and he yelled at them, words which were howled so incoherently he didn't fully understand them himself even as he spoke them. For a moment time seemed to slow, and Jamie felt the air around him grow heavy and thick, before with another yell, he raised his hand, aiming it in the direction of the door.

A blue fire surrounded him, before it exploded outwards in a burst of Power which sent all of the guards flying backwards. They landed on the floor, unconscious.

He only took a moment to wonder what exactly he had managed to do, before he rushed forward and pulled the door open so hard the frame splintered.

Beyond the door was one man who stood at a window.

In the room beyond the glass he could see Sam, unconscious and tied to a large metal pole, the chains wrapped around her body the only things keeping her upright. The image of her there brought about a sickening sense of déjà vu which Jamie decided to ignore, prioritising this situation for now.

Before the man had a chance to fully turn and face the now broken door, Jamie rushed forward, knocking his body into the man's and dragging him to the ground.

But by the time he had the man pinned to the floor it was too late; the flames of the pyre had already begun to burn, he could feel the heat of them on his back and see the glow of them shining through the window.

He couldn't sense Sam anymore.

Bearing his teeth, twisting his mouth into a snarl that would have put the wildest of animals to shame, he looked down at the man and roared, "Turn it off!"

The man simply stared up at Jamie, seeming more awestruck than fearful. His voice barely a whisper, he mumbled just one word.

"James?"

CHAPTER 34

There was a moment of pause, in which Jamie did nothing but stare open-mouthed at the man beneath him, wondering how he could know his name.

Images flashed through his mind, memories from so long ago he'd never given any thought to them until this moment. The blue eyes he now stared into, the once pale face, now slightly tanned through years—*centuries*—of sunlight, and aged at least a decade, yet still familiar to him.

His grip on the man loosened.

Malachi, he thought, his brain still numbed through shock.

Swiftly he pushed himself to his feet and stumbled backwards.

The man stood, never breaking eye contact, and he stared at Jamie as though in a state of shock. "James," he repeated, taking a step forward and reaching out with his hand.

Jamie stopped, his body jolting slightly as his back hit the wall.

Suddenly aware of where he was and remembering why he had come, he turned his attention to the room that lay beyond this one. Ignoring the man, he moved towards the window where there was a room with a circular metal grate, out of which flames still protruded. "Sam," he mumbled, as he strained to make out her shape within the fire, though knowing through his senses that she wasn't there.

The presence of a hand on his shoulder made him jump, and he turned back to the man. "Turn it off," Jamie snarled, feeling his hands curl into fists by his sides. "Stop the fire *now!*"

"James, you don—"

"Stop calling me that!" he ordered, slapping the man's hand away. He took a step forward, the man backed up, seeming afraid. "And turn *off* the fire!"

After a moment of hesitation, the man clicked his fingers, still not taking his eyes off Jamie who turned just in time to see the flames extinguish, leaving nothing behind but a room filled with smoke.

"Where is she?" Jamie demanded.

The man simply stood, gazing at him with an expression akin to disappointment. "You don't remember me?" he spoke quietly. "It is you, isn't it? It's *me*," he continued. "Mal—"

"Stop it," Jamie snapped, glaring at the man, Warlock, Demon . . . whatever he called himself. "How much of a fool do you take me for? If you wanted to wear the face of my brother you should have chosen the one he had when I knew him. Do you think that I don't know about creatures who can wear the faces of others? Now stop the act and tell me what you've done with Sam, tell me or I'll—"

"It's *me*," the man insisted. "I'm *me*. I'm not a Shifter, it's not a glamour. And you," he laughed slightly, "you're a Vampire! When did *that* happen . . . why didn't you come find me?"

"Because you're dead!" he yelled. "Everyone is dead, and you, if you were really my brother you, would know that you were the first to die! Now tell me what you've done with Sam!"

"I haven't done anything with her," he replied, gazing through the window at the now empty room. "I tried to kill her, but obviously her body's not there so she must have found some way to escape."

Jamie stared through the glass, his jaw clenched and his eyes glaring as his fist tightened, the man's words repeating in his mind. *'I tried to kill her.'* He'd said it so casually, as though there wasn't a single thing wrong with what he was saying.

Slowly he faced the man, gazing at him steadily. "You tried to kill her," he stated.

The imposter watched Jamie for a moment, obviously seeing the intent in his eyes, and slowly he began to back away. Raising his hands, palms out in an attempt to show he meant no harm. "She's not dead though," he said, his voice calm and pleading. "She's escaped."

Jamie continued moving towards him. "That doesn't change the fact that you tried."

Without wasting another second, his attempts at pacification forgotten, the man flicked his wrist and a ball of energy flew in Jamie's direction. He managed to duck out of the way before it hit, and instead it flew right past and smashed into the wall behind.

The man fled from the room. With an irritated sigh Jamie ran after him, knowing that even though this man had access to Magic, he didn't have access to the type of speed that Jamie did. It didn't take much effort to catch up to him, as he had barely made it halfway down the hall before Jamie was able to grab hold. And once he came close enough he pounced, knocking the man to the ground once more.

With one hand wrapped in the man's shirt, holding him down as he struggled to break free, he raised his other arm back, putting as much of his strength into this fist as he could. Knowing that if he wished it, he could kill with a single punch.

"Stop!" someone screamed from behind him.

Jamie didn't bother to turn around. He glared down at the man, ready to kill.

The man looked up at him with an expression that was filled with fear. His eyes pleading as he said, "James, please, don't do this. You're my baby brother."

Jamie's jaw clenched, his veins burning with fury as this man dared to speak more lies. "No," Jamie replied through gritted teeth. "My brother is dead."

He brought his fist down swiftly, though before he managed to make impact he was hit with something that knocked him backwards, causing his grip on the man to loosen. He tumbled to the side and landed sprawled on the ground.

He turned his head swiftly, glaring in the direction from which the blast had come, finding Madison standing at the other end of the hallway. The man stumbled to his feet and ran to her, grabbing her by the hand and attempting to pull her away. She didn't move, instead pulling herself free of the imposter's grip and turning to glare at Jamie as he was glaring at her.

Slowly he got to his feet and began making his way towards them. Intent on finishing off the both of them if necessary.

Though before he had a chance to reach them, Danny appeared, with Jade walking in behind. Jamie froze when he saw them standing there, the sudden pause of movement giving pause to his thoughts. He turned and looked over his shoulder, where there lay six unconscious men. He gazed down at his own hands in confusion, his mind feeling slightly muddled as his confused mix of emotions overwhelmed him.

"Where's Sam?" Danny asked, looking at Jamie expectantly.

He snapped his attention to Danny and gazed at him before his eyes drifted in the direction of the Warlock who had taken her.

Apparently, the expression on his face spoke volumes as Danny turned from Jamie and stepped up to the Warlock, shoving him rather aggressively back against the wall. "Where the fuck is my sister?"

"Malachi," Madison said sternly. Jamie's ears pricked at the sound of that name. *Is it really him?* "What have you done with her?"

The Warlock — Malachi — stared at Madison for a brief second, then slowly moved his gaze in Jamie's direction. "She killed Kraven," he said softly. "She's out of control." He turned back to Madison. "She has to be stopped before she kills anyone else."

Madison let a sigh and put a hand to her head. "I told you to back off."

"I know, bu —"

"Where is she?" Madison interrupted. "I swear, if you've killed her —"

"I don't know where she is," he replied. "She somehow managed to escape."

"Jack," Jade said. Everyone turned to look at her. "Did no one else notice that he's not here? He must have Ghost-zapped in then Ghost-zapped them both out."

"Jack?" Malachi asked, gazing at Jade in confusion.

"He probably took her home," Danny said. He grabbed hold of Malachi and shoved him forward. "You're coming with us. And if we can't find her, I swear to the Gods, *I* will kill you."

CHAPTER 35

*I*t was dark.

So dark that Sam couldn't see. Slowly she reached her hands outwards, groping at the cold, heavy air that surrounded her in an attempt to feel where she was.

There was nothing.

At least not anything solid.

She placed her hands on the ground, only to find that there wasn't one. There was nothing but air beneath her. The same cold, heavy emptiness which seemed to surround her on all sides.

Her mind began to whir with panic as the sense of exposure overwhelmed her.

Just as she was about to scream with the frustration of it all, a hand took hold of hers.

A small hand, like that of a child, touched her gently. The fingers entwining with hers, sending a steady flow of calming energy into her body.

"Where am I?" she asked, still unable to see where she was, or who was with her.

"You're in the void," a female voice replied. "The void at the end of your world. Jack tried to send you to Limbo, but I felt that you would be safer here. This is a place that none can see."

"But *I* can't see," Sam whispered. "Who are you? Why did you take me here? Where's Jamie? . . . I was just talking to him and then—"

"Everyone is safe, and you can only see if I show you."

"You did this!" Sam shrieked, wanting to grab hold of the person who held her, but unable to make herself. "You did this to me!"

"Sam," the girl spoke calmly. "Please, there's no time for bickering or for panic. We only have a little time. You don't need to see, you need to listen."

"I don't understand . . . why—"

"You need to keep him safe."

"What? Keep who safe?"

"The Vampire," the girl stated. "You need to keep him safe. They think he is nothing, they don't realise how important he is. But they have plans for you Sam. Bad plans."

"Who—"

"Just listen," the girl snapped, speaking quickly. "He's tainted now. But if you push him away you will die. You need him, he is the *only* one who can save you."

"But—"

"No," the girl interrupted. "Listen. He is the *only* loophole you have. He can be your salvation, but if he dies, we *all* die. You need to keep him safe. You need to keep him strong."

"But . . . " Sam shook her head. "I don't understand."

But the girl moved her hand away, leaving Sam alone once more.

After a few moments of nothing, a light began to appear. It was nothing more than a silver spec at first, hovering in the distance, glowing faintly like a tiny star. But then more began to appear, fading into existence slowly, and soon enough the empty space around her was filled with these strange glowing lights.

The ground beneath her, though it was still nothing but solid black in colour, was hard and unyielding, a solid surface once more. Slowly, Sam pushed herself upright, letting a sigh of relief when she was able to stand and feel something concrete beneath her feet.

She walked towards the lights in front of her. As she came within touching distance of one of the silver orbs, she reached out her hand, attempting to grab hold of it. As her hand phased through the light, a shock of energy shot through her arm, leaving her feeling chilled inside. With a startled jump, she moved away.

"Sam!"

She turned swiftly in the direction of the voice, overcome with relief when she saw Jack running towards her.

"Thank the Gods," he said when he reached her, grabbing hold and pulling her into a tight hug. "I thought I'd lost you on the journey, which would have been *very* bad."

"The journey?" Sam moved away and looked around the space once more. "Where exactly have we journeyed to?"

A smile spread across Jack's face, and he indicated to the room—if it was a room—with his hands. "Welcome to Limbo," he declared proudly.

"Shit!" Sam cried, clutching her chest in search of a pulse. "Am I dead?"

"No, no." Jack grabbed onto her hand and patted it in an attempt at comfort. He laughed a little. "Don't worry, you're not dead. But you are injured. So I pulled your soul out of your body and brought it here while you healed. It's the same thing I did last time, but I don't think you remember it."

For a moment Sam just stared. *Last time?* She thought hard about the last time she had died. Somewhere in her memories she found an image of this place, and though she couldn't fully remember there was a sense of recognition. "You know, it does seem kinda familiar here."

Jack smiled. "Souls are funny that way . . . they remember *everything,* but once they're inside of a body the memories go subconscious and remembering isn't as easy. But the memories can come in dreams sometimes." He looked at her intently for a moment, then sighed. "You know, that's where déjà vu comes from. Memories that you forgot, or memories from another life . . . or in some instances, another soul."

" . . . Okay," Sam replied slowly, not sure what else to say. She knew that Jack was trying to make conversation to take her mind off the fact that she was in a plane of existence meant solely for the dead, but the rambling wasn't helping. With a sigh, she turned her attention to the emptiness of their surroundings. "So where are all the Ghosts, or souls, or whatever?"

Jack pointed to one of the glowing lights. "You're standing in the middle of them," he stated. "This is what the souls of the dead look like. When people die, their souls become energy and then they come here where they wait to be cleansed before being reborn."

"But," Sam looked to Jack, "if that's what dead people look like, then wha . . . "

She let her sentence trail off as she watched Jack and saw how he was staring at her.

A look of dread on his face as though he was preparing himself for the impact of physical pain.

"Then what?" he asked, watching her carefully.

Sam sighed and shrugged. "Nothing, never mind."

After a moment of silence, Jack declared, "I'm gonna go tell everyone where you are so they don't start any more trouble. Wait right there."

He was gone before Sam had a chance to ask where exactly he thought she could go.

CHAPTER 36

*D*anny kept a firm grip on Malachi's arm as Madison opened a portal to take them home.

Jamie stayed back, not wanting to get involved in the situation.

Somewhere in his mind he knew that the Warlock was being truthful; somewhere in his mind he *knew* it was his brother. And although he also knew he should have been happy at the discovery that he was no longer alone, that he still had family alive in the world, he felt nothing.

His anger had subsided and he had been hit by the full realisation of what he'd just done. He stared at the ground, purposely blanking all thoughts from his mind as he didn't want to think about the meaning of his actions, or how they had even been possible.

Jamie was so lost in the nothingness of his own mind that he physically jumped when Jack appeared from nowhere.

He stood next to the portal that Madison had just finished

conjuring and looked at each person one at a time, his eyes lingering on Malachi for slightly longer than anyone else. It looked as though the Warlock was about to speak, but Jack looked away, gazing straight at Jamie as though his words were meant only for him, and said, "Sam's fine. I brought her home."

Jamie let a breath that he only just realised he'd been holding and rushed through the portal, not stopping to listen to the shouts and protests that came from behind. As soon as his feet hit the concrete outside of Sam's house he moved forward, straight up the driveway, through the door and into the house.

Jack materialised on top of the landing, standing in his way.

"She's unconscious," Jack stated. "Probably will be for a while."

He paused on the stairs for a moment, looking over his shoulder when he heard the others arrive. "He tried to kill her," Jamie stated.

Jack let a heavy sigh and leaned back against the wall, his arms folded across his chest. "S'not the first time. He'll probably try again later."

"I almost killed *him*."

Jack shrugged. "I'm sure you're not the only one who's ever tried. A lot of people think he's a dick."

Jamie gazed in Jack's direction and said quietly, "He's my . . . he's my brother."

For a moment Jack simply stared, then slowly his expression darkened. His brow creasing and his lips set in a harsh line. He pushed himself away from the wall, his body now wedged between Jamie and the hallway leading to Sam's room. "Your brother is leader of the Underworld? Strange how in the past four months *that* never came into conversation."

Jamie clenched his jaw, trying—and failing—not to be insulted by the obvious accusation being thrown at him. "That's because before ten minutes ago I thought he was dead."

"You seem to think that about a lot of people," Jack mumbled, his eyes glaring.

With an irritated huff, Jamie pushed past him and stormed into Sam's room, slamming the door behind him and leaning his back against it momentarily. He let a sigh and looked up, staring at Sam lying curled up on her bed.

His breath caught in his throat at the sight of her, his brain not wanting to process what his eyes were seeing.

But there was no way he could not. The image of Sam lying in her bed, her skin charred and peeling, pieces of it burnt to what appeared to be ash, the rest of her enflamed and blistered, would be forever imprinted into his memories.

For a good while he could do nothing but stare at her, wondering if that even *was* her, and after the image of her had truly settled into his mind and he accepted the fact that it was indeed Sam, he began to wonder if she felt any pain or if the fire had burned her nerves to the stage that her body was numbed.

Or was the fact that she was currently in a magically educed coma helping whatever pain she may have been feeling subside to a barely noticeable point?

Or, like before, was her body once again somehow empty?

These and many other thoughts and worries flooded through Jamie's mind all at once, making his chest ache, as though he was drowning within his own body.

He took a breath and forced himself to move to her, wanting to do what he could to speed up her healing. Wanting her to be well, but more importantly awake.

He needed Sam to explain what was happening to him.

As he reached her bed he sat down on the mattress beside her, ensuring that his movements were slow and gentle so as not to move her in any way that may cause further discomfort.

Slowly, he reached a shaking hand towards her, about to touch it to her face. But he froze as his stomach clenched at the thought of touching her damaged skin. His fingers were less than an inch from her cheek when he pulled his hand away and held it in front of himself, gazing with unseeing eyes at the lines on his hands. His eyes suddenly focused as he caught sight of the miniscule blue veins that entwined beneath his skin.

Without giving too much thought to what could happen to Sam if his blood were to mix with hers—focusing solely on the fact that he knew his blood was capable of healing—he brought his wrist to his mouth and bit down on the softest part, right where the veins entwined, only pulling away when the blood flowed onto his tongue.

Gently, he reached his other arm forward and slid it under Sam's head. His breath held, filling up his chest with unnecessary oxygen, he pulled her to his chest and placed his wrist to her lips.

CHAPTER 37

$\mathcal{S}$am felt light and heavy all at the same time.

It was like the feeling you'd get when falling asleep; that sensation of floating and falling all at once.

Breathing was easy.

So easy that she felt as though she was suffocating in the air she consumed. But when she tried to focus on trying to breathe right she couldn't.

So instead she focused on waking up.

But when she opened her eyes she noticed the strangest thing . . .

She could see herself.

Except it wasn't her.

Not really.

Not anymore.

Somehow she was now two, the body and the Power. She could see her body which meant that she—the she that was no longer physical—must have been the Power. Somehow she had been separated from the thing that kept her solid, the thing that kept her bound to this plane of existence.

With a feeling that was difficult to identify she looked on as the doors opened and a man was dragged inside. She watched as the man that she had loved, the one she had shared her body, her life and her soul with was dragged into the room, his wrists bound in chains. She looked on as he fought, as he screamed and pleaded and begged for her body to be saved.

He didn't know that she was no longer there.

He didn't know that she couldn't be saved.

None of them could.

She could now see everything so clearly.

All that was.

All that is.

All that had to be.

And that was when she knew that they could not be saved.

When the others were brought in and the flames began she saw *him* . . . no, not him, she realised with a start . . . *her*. She could see it so clearly now, the feeling of hate that had warped this feminine soul into nothing more than an oozing shadow that reeked of anger, hatred and an uncontrollable lust for vengeance.

Kon.

That was her name.

Chaos.

That was her entity.

All that was and all that wasn't.

Sam watched her as she stood, wrapped in the cloak of Shadows that allowed her to see without actually being there, and immediately Sam knew why they would all die.

She knew it was their fate.

A fate they had brought upon themselves.

A fate which would haunt their bloodlines until the blood ran no more . . .

CHAPTER 38

Jamie's blood helped to speed up the healing. Most of Sam's scars vanished within a few minutes, and any others were gone soon after. It didn't take longer than ten minutes in total before Sam looked like herself again.

Her fingers twitched and her eyelids fluttered rapidly, almost as though she were caught within a nightmare. For a few moments Jamie simply watched, wondering where she was and whether or not he would have to go back inside her mind to wake her.

With a sigh he looked towards the door, wondering how long it would be before the others barged in. He listened carefully, and was relieved to find that everyone was downstairs arguing about the Warlock. They seemed distracted enough not to bother with either him or Sam for quite a while.

He looked down at her, still unconscious but not looking comfortable.

Unwilling to wait for his answers and knowing how much Sam hated questions and most likely wouldn't answer anyway, he placed his hand on her forehead and sent a bolt of his Power into her.

She gasped and sat up quite suddenly. Surprised at how quickly his intrusion had awoken her, he placed his hand more firmly on her head and tried to force her back down. She struggled, her eyelids fluttering rapidly as she did. When he sent the second jolt of energy through her, that was when she opened her eyes and let out a Power blast of her own.

The energy caught him off guard, picking him up and pushing him across the room, his back hitting into the wall.

She looked in his direction, her lips slightly parted as though she was caught between a feeling of shock and confusion. Slowly she moved her hand to her head and said between her teeth, "What the fuck is *wrong* with you?"

Jamie got to his feet, never taking his eyes off her. "I was just trying to wake you u—"

"Bullshit," she interrupted. "You were trying to keep me incapacitated. You think I haven't used that kind of energy enough to know what it feels like?"

With a sigh he leaned his back against her door. "I wasn't trying to keep you incapacitated. Why would I do something like that?"

"I don't know," Sam said sarcastically, glaring at him. "Why *would* you do something like that?"

He glared at her, his teeth clenched. "Don't be so fucking paranoid."

Her expression changed so suddenly, her eyes widening in shock as she stared right at him. He watched her carefully, confused by her sudden change in demeanour.

Sam pushed herself off the bed and walked to him quickly, grabbing his chin with one hand and bringing his eyes level with hers. "What—"

"Shut up," she said, her expression serious, her eyes assessing.

Hesitantly, she let him go and took a step back, still gazing at him strangely.

"What!" he exclaimed in frustration. "What is it *now*? What do you think is wrong with me now? Do you think I'm trying to hurt you?" He grabbed her by the shoulders and shook her. "Tell me!"

She smacked him on the chest and he let her go. "You tell me. You're the one who's been acting weird. So just tell me. Maybe I can help—"

"Help what? Help me control my sudden ability to shoot Magic at people? Or maybe you want to explain it all to me? Oh but that's right, you don't like to answer people's questions. You don't *like* to talk to people. You just want everyone to leave you alone forever. I know you have the answers in there." He placed his finger on her forehead. "I thought I'd save us both the tiring effort of talking by just taking what I need from you, since I know you did this me. See, I finally figured out that it's you . . . *You're* my problem."

Sam took a small step away from him. "Your what?"

He laughed humourlessly. "Oh don't act so naïve . . . you're not the only one who's life was fine before we met. I don't know what you've done to me this time, maybe you're trying to drive me insane because of what I said to you. I won't take it back, you know."

"Jamie—"

"Shut up Sam, I don't want to hear anything else from you. I don't want any more of your blame or your accusations or your whining, or your 'poor *me*, why does everything bad happen to *me*, why does everyone try to kill *me*'. Just stop it and reverse whatever you did to make this happen!"

Jamie breathed heavily as he watched her jaw clench, her fury evident by the crackling glow in her eyes. "Tell me what exactly I'm supposed to have done to you, what exactly have I made happen?"

He let a huff and walked up to her, sure to invade her personal space. "You put something inside my head. A whisper, a thought, a dream . . . I don't know what, you're the one who put it there. And since you put it there things have been happening and I don't know how to make it stop. So *you* make it stop."

She took a deep breath and sat down on the edge of her bed. "Has this dream been keeping you awake?"

For a moment he gazed at her curiously, wondering why she was asking questions that she should already know the answers to. But after that moment of curiosity had passed he felt his anger return. And he knelt on the bed beside her, moving his face just inches from hers. "Was that your plan?" he asked. "Did you try to get in my head Sam? Try to do to me what you did to Scott? All because I didn't want you anymore?"

"I thought you were immune to my Magic . . . you said so yourself, right?"

"You must have found a way—"

She rolled her eyes and scoffed. "When *exactly* do you think I had the time to do that? To find a way inside your head I'd have to spend a lot of time trying. And in case you didn't notice, until last night you weren't talking to me. When did it start, huh? Was it this morning? Last night? A day ago? A week ago? A month ago? When Jamie? When did you stop being able to sleep?"

With a sigh he sat back, running his hand through his hair as he thought. "It happened the night I killed you . . . I think that was the first time I dreamt it."

"What did you dream?" she asked, placing her hand on his.

He looked her in the eyes for a moment, a strange feeling stirring within the pit of his stomach as he felt suddenly able to see with such clarity it made him wonder when his mind had become fogged.

Slowly he moved away, watching Sam as though seeing her for the first time. Under her concerned gaze, the weight of everything that had happened hit him with such force he felt ready to break. He took his hand away, and ran it through his hair. When his fingers caught in the tangled mess he realised he couldn't remember the last time he'd washed it and the more he tried to think the more blanks he found in his memory. "God Sam, I'm sorry."

"What?"

He stood, looking down at the clothes he couldn't remember dressing himself in. "I'm so sorry, I don't know what's happening to me. I feel like I'm going mad."

She grabbed onto his hand, holding onto it tightly, forcing him to turn so he would face her. "Tell me what you dreamt."

"It's different every time, but still the same . . . there's a cell and I'm chained. Then there's this room, and all these people and so many Shadows, and then . . . "

"And then what?"

" . . . and then you die, and I can't stop it. I try, every time I try but I can't and it just keeps happening again and again. And I don't think it's a dream. It feels — it just feels so real. And then when I wake up I don't — I don't know. I just . . . I don't know."

"It's okay," she said, loosening her grip on his hand, lightly stroking her thumb along his skin in an attempt at comfort. "We'll figure out what's happening to you and find a way to fix it. Just, I mean, you know that I didn't do this to you, right?" Jamie looked at her, she gazed at him with apprehension, but despite her obvious anxiety he could tell by the openness of her expression and the emotion reflected in her eyes that she wasn't lying.

Whatever was happening, Sam wasn't responsible for it.

Slowly, he nodded his head. "I know."

"Good." She took her hand from his and stood. "The last thing I need is *more* people trying to kill me. Speaking of which, is Jack around? He needs to explain to me what happened and who needs to pay for it."

"Wait!" Jamie rushed to the door and slammed it shut before she had a chance to leave. She jumped back slightly, her eyes wide and startled.

"What?"

"Uh . . . there's something that I need to talk to you about before you go out there."

Sam looked at him expectantly for a moment, then let an irritated sigh. *"What?"*

"It's the man, the one who . . . who *burned* you. I'm not sure *how* . . . I thought that he was dead, but as it turns out he's not dead, and I don't know how because I mean it's been so —"

"You're rambling." Sam let a heavy breath and placed her hands on her hips. "If there's a point can you get to it sometime today? There's a lot of shit we really need to deal with."

Jamie glared, clenching his jaw with anger at being interrupted. "He's my brother."

He watched her face carefully for countless moments, trying to judge her thoughts by her expression.

The process proved to be quite difficult as so far she'd managed to keep her face surprisingly neutral.

It seemed like an eternity passed in which she just stood there watching him, before she finally spoke, "So . . . your *brother* is the guy who's been trying to kill me since, forever?

And you didn't think that this *brother* of yours was worth mentioning before right now?"

Jamie opened his mouth to explain the situation slightly clearer, but Sam held up a hand to silence him. "There's only one question that you need to answer, and it will tell me everything that I need to know. What would you do if I hunted him down right now and killed him?"

Without a moment of hesitation, Jamie looked her directly in the eyes and said, "Nothing."

His answer seemed to surprise her more than it evoked any other response, which he found to be slightly confusing. Why should his answer be surprising? What had she expected him to say?

Without an ounce of humour in his tone, he let a small laugh. "Why *would* I care? I've spent years thinking he was dead so it wouldn't make much difference to me if he actually was. So if you want to kill him, go ahead, I won't stop you. And by the way, I don't appreciate the accusation you thought at me." He opened the door and stormed out into the hallway, calling over his shoulder, "I only wanted you to hear it from me first."

He stomped down the stairs, not needing to look back to know that Sam was following him. Everyone was standing in the living room, all facing Malachi who was the only one sitting. They all turned in his direction as he walked into the room. Without stopping to explain himself or saying a word at all, he twisted his hand in Malachi's jumper and pulled him to his feet then threw him across the room where he landed sprawled at Sam's feet.

Jamie glared at her for a moment, as Malachi — seeming more than slightly worried — scrambled to a more upright position. "No hunting needed," he said to her, directing towards the Warlock. "What are you waiting for? You said you wanted to kill him."

"James . . . " Malachi looked at him with an expression of hurt.

"Shut up," he snapped. "This doesn't concern you."

Madison stepped forward, grabbing Malachi by the hand and pulling him backwards.

Sam stepped forward slowly, her steady gaze penetrating. "You would really let me kill your brother?"

"Like I said," he smirked, "it makes *no* difference to me."

CHAPTER 39

$\mathcal{A}$leczander was starting to feel as though wandering through the realm of mortals was becoming quite the regular occurrence.

So much so, that when he'd received the text message from Jamie asking to meet him he hadn't thought twice about leaving the kingdom and venturing outside alone. Whereas less than a month ago it would have been something he'd been wary of, and then only agree to if he did not go alone.

It wasn't as though he feared for his safety in this world. It was simply a matter of custom and that it had not been a part of his to venture outside.

After he received the message from Jamie asking to meet, he had attempted to call, wondering if it was a matter that could be discussed over the phone. But when there had been no answer he had grown concerned enough to come alone to Jamie's home. Knowing that there were some matters that were better discussed in person and thinking that perhaps there were things Jamie needed to discuss with someone that he could not discuss with Sam.

Although Aleczander loved Sam as though she were his own flesh and blood he was not blind to her shortcomings. And he understood that genuine heart to heart conversations had never been a strong suit of hers.

He approached the house slowly, his body freezing unexpectedly as he cleared the trees that surrounded the house. He turned his head upwards, his eyesight good enough to allow him to see the runes which burned brightly on the trees around the house, invisible to those less attuned to the energies of the worlds around them. Aleczander smiled to himself, knowing it was Sam who had put them there and also recognising that he could step no further without an invitation from the owner of the home.

He reached his hand into the pocket of his coat and pulled out his phone, attempting to call Jamie once more.

Nearby he heard a phone ringing, and knew without concentrating that the sound was not coming from inside the house, it was coming from behind him.

Before he had a chance to look over his shoulder, a needle was jammed into his neck.

CHAPTER 40

$\mathcal{S}$am punched him so hard she felt something break.

At first she wasn't sure if it was his nose or her knuckles, but when he looked at her and she saw the blood streaming down his face she knew that it hadn't been herself she'd injured.

His eyes burned as he glared at her; she saw Magic spark within them, saturating the normally icy blue, giving them an otherworldly vibrancy.

There was still no darkness—no *Shadows*—within them, only a Magic that he shouldn't have possessed.

Jamie wiped the blood off his face, his nose healing itself within a matter of seconds. He stared at the red stain on his hand for a moment, then laughed though there was no humour in its tone.

"Sam?" Jack queried from behind. She only held up her hand in response. Not looking over her shoulder to face him. Not thinking an explanation in his direction. Not so much as whispering a syllable.

And Jack didn't question her further, understanding that she was doing something necessary and that she would explain what she could when she could.

Jamie licked at the blood that stained his upper lip before wiping away the rest. Slowly he looked up from the stains and for the umpteenth time in the past few days Sam saw *that* expression in his eyes. The one that told her this was not the Jamie she knew, this was someone – something – else entirely. The one that made her feel as though she was staring into the face of a stranger.

In less than a few seconds, happening so quickly it was barely a noticeable transition, his look of amusement turned to one of fury. The air became inundated with the heavy feeling of strong Magic. The lights flickered, and as they did Sam saw the streetlamps outside follow suit.

When the lights came back on, so did everything else – the stereo, the TV, the lamps, various kitchen appliances – all were charged externally by an uncontrolled supernatural Power.

A Power beyond that of any Vampire.

She didn't need to turn to the others to know that they were all slowly coming to the same realisation that had been nagging at Sam's mind for the past few days.

Jamie wasn't Jamie anymore.

In a movement so fast Sam barely had enough time to react, he lunged at her. His body slamming into hers so hard she fell backwards. Someone moved behind and caught her before she hit into the wall or any of the furniture. She looked up to find Danny at her back, his hands placed firmly on her shoulders, his eyes glaring at Jamie, who stood in the centre of the room watching her with an expression of malignant glee.

"The fuck is your problem?" Danny asked, letting go of

Sam and stepping forward. She could tell by his body language that he was preparing himself for a fight.

Jamie just watched him.

Not answering.

Not moving.

Just watching and smiling.

Sam grabbed onto Danny's arm and pulled him back so he was standing next to her. He looked at her quizzically. "Don't," she said. "Leave him alone."

"What's going on?" Malachi asked, looking from Jamie to Sam, then Danny and back again. "What's—"

"Don't," Jade cut him off, shaking her head. She caught Sam's eyes and gave her the look. The *'I understand what's happening and what we need to do'* look. Sam gave a small nod in her direction.

Sam stepped forward, walking slowly in a circle around Jamie as he continued to observe her.

"You asked me a question," he said. "You shouldn't lash out at me just because you don't like my answer."

She continued to move around him, and he turned his body to follow her, ensuring that he could keep her in his sights. "And you shouldn't lash out at me just because I lash out at you."

He laughed a little. "Have you ever heard the expression, you get what you give?"

She stopped when he had his back to the others and raised an eyebrow at him. "So basically you're claiming the whole 'you started it' thing? Very mature."

His smile faded quickly and he glared. "*You* want to talk to *me* about being ma—"

His sentence was cut off when Jack attacked him from behind. He'd managed to move towards Jamie unnoticed and snap his neck with the quick precision and skill gained from years of training.

Jack held onto Jamie once his body had gone limp and gently placed him on the floor. Arranging him in a way that he would be comfortable.

He stood and let a sigh. "Alright. That will take him at *least* an hour to heal."

CHAPTER 41

or a few moments Malachi did nothing, only stood in the corner of the room, stunned silent and too confused to think of how he should react. It was only when he saw Sam kneel by his brother's side and reach her hand out to touch his skin that he felt anger spur him on and he rushed in her direction, jaw clenched in anger.

"What have you done to him!" he yelled, just as the blonde man-Witch grabbed onto his arm and pulled him back, keeping him restrained and away from Sam.

Sam didn't even seem to register that he'd spoken, or if she did had not cared enough to pay attention. She reached her fingers out to James and pressed them against his neck, probing at the skin in various places as though examining the damage.

With a sigh she stood and looked to Jack. "He's already healing. Faster than usual. We'll need to chain him up quickly."

"Chain him up?" Madison asked, looking around the room.

Malachi could tell by the expression on the faces of the other people in the room that he and Madison were the only two confused by the situation.

He didn't speak again, noting by the way Sam regarded Madison that she seemed more willing to acknowledge her presence than she was his, and realising that his best chance at having his questions answered was to allow Madison to do the talking.

Sam stared at Madison for a moment, then folded her arms and let a sigh. "Yes. We need to chain him up before he hurts anyone."

"Um . . . okay."

Sam walked towards the door. Everyone else stayed put, all except for Madison who followed her. "I know that I don't know him that well, but is he always like that? Because he was pretty nice to me the first time I met him."

"The *first* time you met him? You knew that my brother was alive and you didn't think to tell me?"

Madison looked at him over her shoulder, and shrugged. "How was I supposed to know you were related?"

Sam rolled her eyes and turned her back to the room, moving quickly out of sight.

From his right he heard Jade let a long heavy sigh before she walked forward and let herself fall onto the sofa. She leaned back and seemed to look in his direction, but when she spoke he realised she wasn't looking at him but at the man-Witch who was still holding onto his arm. "This day is stressing me out. Tell me you grabbed some snack foods."

"I was a bit busy, you know, with the whole trying to track you down thing."

Jade huffed and closed her eyes. "This day is officially the worst."

Faster than Malachi had expected, Sam returned, her arms burdened with a long and heavy chain. At first it was all he noticed until she raised her other hand and threw something through the air. He watched the glass vial sail over his shoulder and turned to find the man-Witch holding what was surely a potion. He gazed at it curiously, as did the man-Witch, who then looked to Sam. "What's this?"

Sam nodded in Malachi's direction. "I only have one set of chains."

That seemed to be all the explanation that was needed, and before Malachi had a chance to get on the same page everyone else seemed to be on, he was pushed to his knees. Jack was holding him down, two hands placed firmly on his shoulders and the man-Witch's hand was tangled in his hair, pulling his head back so far he was gazing straight into the light on the ceiling.

Before he had a chance to struggle, the other hand came down and slammed the vial to his lips, forcing the potion down his throat.

It was an odd sensation . . . a cold tingling. He tried his best not to swallow, but his head was held back until every last drop was gone. Once the vial was empty he was released by his captors. He leaned forward and coughed, pushing his breaths into his stomach in the hopes that he could perhaps make himself sick and rid his body of the poison he'd just been fed.

Malachi turned his glare in Sam's direction, about to demand an explanation, but before he opened his mouth Madison screamed in quite a hysterical tone, "What the fuck did you do to him?"

Sam gave a small smile as she knelt beside James, wrapping the chains around both his wrists and ankles. "Chill," she said. "It's only a binding potion. It'll wear off by the time

Jamie is done with these chains."

Malachi clenched his jaw at the way Sam spoke about his brother, using the pet name only their mother had used for him. As if she had a right to refer to him in such a way.

Instead of speaking his grievances aloud, he simply watched as Madison looked momentarily in his direction before taking a hesitant step closer to Sam. "Why does he even *need* the chains?" she queried, before she asked the question that Malachi truly wanted an answer to. "What's wrong with him?"

He felt a shift in the aura of the room before he even saw the transformation of expression on the faces of the others and it was obvious by the adjustment of Madison's demeanour that she could feel the change too.

Sam let a sigh and stood looking as though she was the one about to answer. But the response came from Jack who was still standing behind him. "Jamie's been . . . different, lately."

"I keep thinking that maybe he's been possessed by the same thing that's been getting everyone else, the same thing that got him before." Sam looked down at James and let another sigh. "But that's not it because the physical signs aren't there, so I don't know what's wrong. There's only one other theory I have, but I don't know how I can find out for sure, or even how to fix him when I do find out. So I guess, for now, the best thing is to keep him chained up so he doesn't hurt anyone."

That was when it happened.

The laughter.

It was a small one at first, a chuckle really, an outward expression of Malachi's disbelief at the information he was receiving. But it quickly became uncontrollable and soon he was laughing loudly. Drawing the attention of everyone in the room. Receiving confused stares from everyone but Sam who seemed only capable of glaring.

"That is the most ridiculous thing I've ever heard!" he declared. "Your method of help is to keep him chained for however long it takes you to come up with an actual plan?"

"And that's funny why?" Jade asked.

"Well darling, it's funny because I realised that I've spent the past few years of my life trying to capture a girl who is incapable of coming up with any viable plan of action and I just find it funny that I've been outsmarted by an imbecile."

Jade smiled slightly. "Says more about you than it does Sam though, doesn't it?"

Madison let a tired sigh and shook her head at him disapprovingly. "What's your other theory?" she asked Sam.

Sam didn't answer for a moment, instead just continued to glare at Malachi. Then slowly she turned her attention to Madison. "He has Magic," she replied. "He shouldn't have Magic like that, he's a Vampire and, well . . . his body wasn't built for it so maybe it's hurting him in some way . . . making him different, you know?"

"But how did he even gain the ability for it in the first place?"

Sam hesitated, looking over Malachi's shoulder to where Jack stood. Jack replied, "There was this unidentified entity that attacked Jamie about a week ago, it possessed him and made him act strangely, kind of the way he has been lately. But Sam said that last time there were physical signs of possession that aren't there now. While he was possessed by that thing, he consumed Sam's blood."

Malachi snorted. "You let a Vampire drink you, like a cheap can of Coke . . . harlot."

Sam paid no mind to his words, but he knew that someone was at least paying attention to him when the man-Witch punched him in the back of the neck, harder than was necessary for a remark like that.

He glared over his shoulder, but the man-Witch had already turned his attention to Jack, and he didn't look happy. "You know, you could have told me *how* she was attacked."

Jack shrugged. "I didn't want to give you another reason to be a dick to him."

The man-Witch turned to Sam. "How much did he drink?"

Sam turned her face away before she answered, "All of it."

CHAPTER 42

$\mathcal{I}$t was quiet for a few minutes after that.

No one said a word, but Sam could feel the stares of those in the room.

Danny was the first to speak. "He drank *all* of your blood?"

Sam huffed, "Yes Danny, he drank *all* of my blood. Now can we please focus on doing something to make him better so that we can deal with our newest problem?"

He scowled in response, then glared and said, "I have a solution. Why don't we just let him die? I volunteer to kill him personally. That's one problem solved. And we can kill this one too. That's two problems solved. And if we act now we can even be done in time for dinner. How's that for a plan?"

Malachi sprang to his feet, freeing himself from both Danny and Jack. He spun around and shoved Danny against the wall, rattling the pictures that hung in their frames. It was the first time Sam had noticed that there were photos on the walls, photos of the family; Danny's parents and grandparents and the two of them as kids. She wondered when he'd put them back up and why he'd bothered.

"No one is killing my brother!" Malachi yelled in Danny's face.

Jack pulled him off, throwing him to the floor. He landed on his ass in the most ungracious of positions. Sam found herself taking mental pictures for when she found a way to print memories and spread them around town.

"No one's killing Jamie," Sam said calmly as she glared at Danny. "We both know I'd rather kill you first. But *you*," Sam slapped the back of Malachi's head. "If you don't shut the fuck up and cooperate I might just kill you. Don't think because I didn't let Jamie do it that I'm against the idea. Because I'm not. Now . . . can we *please* focus on this? He'll be awake soon and I'd rather know what we need to do to fix him before he wakes up and tries to go on a rampage."

"Step one should probably be to find out what's wrong with him exactly," Jade suggested, turning slightly so that she could see Sam over the top of the couch. "Is there a Vampire doctor who could check him out or something?"

Sam shook her head; if it was really as simple as that she would have called Aleczander already and had him deal with it. "I don't think it's Vampire related, I think it's something else. But I don't know what. I don't know a lot about Power absorption or possession. I wouldn't even know where —"

"I know!" Madison yelled, watching Sam eagerly as she spoke with way too much enthusiasm. "We have archives and a whole library filled with records and books and stuff. You could come and look through it. We can help."

"*Excuse* me?" Malachi got to his feet with a dangerous look in his eyes and stared at Madison in disbelief. "Did you just invite our enemies to our home for the second time in one day?"

"They're not our enemies," Madison retorted, placing her hands on her hips as she spoke. "Sam is my friend, and if you were listening to the conversation you would have heard that she's trying to help *your* family. How would you feel knowing that you had information to help save his life —"

"I don't think he's dying," Sam interjected, but Madison held up her hand to silence her.

"You have information to *save his life* and you're just gonna not help? Would you let me die too? What about —"

"He's not dying," Malachi stated. "Apparently he's just ill. And I haven't seen him in a while, how can I be sure that's there's anything wrong with him at all? It could be some kind of trick to get inside the base and kill us all."

"I think if they wanted to kill us they would have done it earlier . . . when they were at the base."

Malachi let a sigh of defeat then glared at Sam. "I will stay with you all the whole time. You will not touch anything that is not made of paper. You will not destroy, damage or steal *anything*."

"Well there goes my evil plan to steal all of your books . . . What ever will I do now?" Sam smiled proudly at herself when she heard Jade laugh.

CHAPTER 43

The room smelled cold.

The air was fresh and heavy and gave his nostrils a dry, cracked feeling when he inhaled.

But it was not the type of cold that would indicate he was still somewhere outside. The lack of any flowing breeze was proof enough that he was not outside.

No. This was the type of cold smell that came from being inside a room with little to no insulation, possibly one made from wood or cinderblock.

Although the air also held the scent of dust and earth. A mixture of natural materials and those which were manmade.

It would have been helpful to be able to see, but Aleczander's eyes were still too heavy to open. His head was limp and relaxed at an awkward angle, made even more uncomfortable by the fact that he was sitting and not lying.

If he had to guess, he would say he was in a room made of brick and concrete. But one far away from the bustle of a city or town. The scent of earth that mingled in the cold air he breathed was indicative of a place in the forest.

But which forest was the question.

Was he home or was he elsewhere?

The sound of creaking hinges broke the silence of the room, and he strained to open his eyes, or turn his head in the direction of the opening door. Fresh air flowed inside, followed by the footsteps of three people, two of which were significantly heavier than the other.

He could tell by the sound and also by the scent of them that two were male and one was female.

The door creaked once more as it closed.

A feeling of heaviness prevented him from making any significant movements, and the slight movements and twitches that he could manage drained him of what little energy he had. With a sigh, he relaxed his body and allowed his head to fall into an even more uncomfortable angle.

His pitiful movements exerting a contemptuous chuckle from his captors.

Light footsteps approached him; the woman moved forward with confident strides and stopped so close that when he breathed in he could feel her very essence and knew without being able to see that she was a Vampire.

A faint smile curved his lips; with that knowledge he knew what he was here for, knew why he had been taken, but also knew exactly how he would survive.

From the very moment she stepped into his presence he could sense everything about her, down to the expression she now wore on her face.

And he knew all of this because she was nothing but a mere Vampire, and he the Vampire King.

CHAPTER 44

$\mathcal{S}$am looked over Jamie's arm as she fixed his chains to the sturdy metal chair Madison had managed to procure. She watched Malachi carefully as he escorted the last of the archivists from the room, watching for any signs of him sounding an alarm. The very last thing she needed or wanted to deal with right now was a mob of angry Warlocks trying to kill her.

The deal she'd made with Malachi was that he could supervise their perusing, untied and free to roam of his own accord under the condition that he cleared the Archive of any of his people first and did all in his power to ensure their safety.

Although he wasn't happy with the arrangement, he eventually agreed, but was sure to let her and everyone know that he was only helping Jamie—or James as he kept calling him—and would kill Sam almost as quickly as she would kill him if there was any funny business.

The large doors closed with a loud echoing thump as the last of the Warlocks left, leaving only Sam, Jack, Jade, Danny, Madison and Malachi in the room with their Vampire hostage.

With a sigh Sam stood and made her way to the centre of the room, taking a moment to gaze around and take in the grandeur of the Archive as briefly as she could before shooting her glare back to Malachi, who watched her just as carefully as she watched him.

"So where do we start?" Jade asked, folding her arms across her chest. She looked to Sam expectantly. "What exactly are we looking for?"

Sam let a sigh. "I guess we're looking for anything on Vampires, or possession. We'll start there."

Jade turned to Malachi. "And how many things on Vampires and possession do you have here?"

He shrugged. "I dunno. I've never done research before."

Jack gaped at him. "What do you mean you've never done research before?"

Malachi regarded Jack in confusion. "That's what we have librarians for. It's their job to know everything, and they just tell you what you need to know."

Sam realised his idiocy made her despise him more.

"What are you glaring at me for?" he asked as he pointed to Sam. "*You're* the one who demanded the room be cleared. If you wanted it to be easy to find things you should have thought your plan through!"

She rolled her eyes and turned her back to him, choosing to face out to the room and regard the ten foot tall shelves that seemed to stretch on for miles. She let a sigh as she moved towards the records. "Everyone spread out and just look through as many things as you can. There has to be a system. Yell when you find the shelf on Vampires and again when you find the one on possession."

Without any more words being exchanged, everyone spread out, each taking separate aisles. All except for Malachi who followed closely behind Sam, glaring at her while she sifted through the manuscripts.

None of the books had titles on the spines, just an eleven digit code that she was sure meant something to someone, but to her they were just a random configuration of meaningless letters and numbers. She pulled a bunch of them from the shelf and flicked through the pages, before realising that they would contain no useful information and placed them back on the shelf.

She gazed down the row of books she had to go through with despair. The line went on so far that it stemmed into shadow and became partially invisible.

The fact that Malachi was doing nothing to help her get through the records faster made her so annoyed that she pulled a manuscript from the shelf and flung it at his head.

He leaned to the side and whacked it out of the way before it hit him, then glared at her, his face flushed red with anger. "We had a deal that neither of us would start a fight."

"We also agreed that you would be helpful," she hissed. "Standing around doing fuck all is *not* helpful."

"I let you in here didn't I?" he snarled through gritted teeth. "What exactly would make you think I'd do anything more to help *you*, murderer."

"Murderer? Do you really think you get to call me names like that after how many of my family *you've* killed?"

"I never harmed anyone you cared about!"

"Fuck you liar!" she screamed, his denial only fuelling her anger.

Malachi's jaw clenched, and he moved forward, his face contorted with anger, his hands balled into fists at his sides.

Feeling almost relieved that there was now cause for violence, Sam responded in kind; she channelled Magic into her hand, readying a projectile to hit him with before he got a chance to hit her.

Before either of them had a chance to throw the first punch, Jack appeared beside Sam and grabbed onto her arm, pulling her aside so roughly she almost fell on her backside. Danny stepped in front of Malachi and shoved him backwards so that he stumbled into one of the shelves.

"Get off me!" Sam yelled, pulling her arm from Jack's grasp. "He started it!"

"Fuck you *harlot*," Malachi screamed. "Who's the fucking liar now?"

Sam whirled on him, trying to move towards him as Jack tried to hold her back.

She was so distracted by her anger that she didn't feel the electric buzz fill the air until it released in a sharp strike of energy.

Sam froze, as did everyone else. Madison and Jade stood behind Danny, staring down the aisle where the Magic had originated from and caused a few books at various places on the shelves to fall to the floor.

For a moment Sam just stared at them curiously, before she turned her gaze in Jack's direction.

He looked at her in confusion, then, obviously seeing the unspoken question in her eyes, raised his hands in agitation. "Oh come *on*. Why is it that every time a book falls to the floor *I* get the blame for it?"

She shrugged. "Who else would behave like a Ghost and use invisible energy to knock things over?"

Jack let a sigh. "There are three other people in the room, and every single one of them looks shifty."

"There's seven of us," Jade stated. "If you include the one

who's unconscious."

"*Exactly!* My point is that any one of you could have done it."

"I never said you did anything!" Sam argued.

"Not out loud you didn't," Jack mumbled as he moved away, walking towards the fallen books picking them up one at a time.

He carried them out of the aisles and over to the table where Jamie was tied to a chair. He let them all drop to the table with a loud bang, and seated himself on one of the other chairs.

Sulking as he began to flick through the pages.

They had spent almost thirty minutes checking through the books that had fallen from the shelves, all agreeing it was as good a place to start as any.

Each of them had taken a book to look through, and Sam, after finding a reference number scrawled inside one of them decided to head back into the shelves to try find the corresponding manuscript.

What she found was a book of records, or more specifically a record of executions from the early seven hundreds.

When her eyes skimmed the text scrawled through the first record, her mind brought her back to the dream she'd had earlier.

The one where she'd been looking down at a room full of people being burned alive.

An execution.

The fine hairs on the back of her neck stood on end at the images flashing through her mind. She flicked through the pages with interest, knowing what she would find before she did.

On the last few pages were a few paragraphs detailing an execution from the early seven hundreds and a list of thirteen names.

Thirteen people that had been sentenced to death.

The book slipped from her hands and hit the floor with a thud as she realised it was real.

Everything she dreamt was real.

CHAPTER 45

"How many are there?" the woman asked.

Aleczander's smile widened, though he did not respond to her question. His eyes were still closed, his body still weighed down by the tranquiliser that flowed through his blood.

Within his mind, he saw as she placed her hands on her hips and scowled. Then began to pace back and forth, frustrated by his lack of response.

Through her eyes he noticed that the two men stood by the door were both armed with guns, crossbows and swords.

He knew from the woman's—Bethany's—thoughts that they were Vampire Hunters. He could tell by the scent of them that they were both afraid, though were forcing an air of bravado to compensate for the obvious.

Bethany stopped pacing suddenly and turned, slapping him across the face with the full force of her strength. She knotted her fingers in his hair and pulled, holding his head upright in her grip. "I know that you're not unconscious enough to be this unresponsive, so *answer me!*"

She let go of his head more roughly than she had held it. "How many are there?" she asked again. "How many have you sired?"

Aleczander said nothing.

Staying silent and unmoving as he allowed his energy to restore and did nothing—not even breathing—in order to build up as much of his energy as he could.

Knowing that it was only a matter of time before he would be strong enough to kill them.

And knowing that she could not and would not kill him without an answer to her question.

She let a belligerent sigh and grabbed onto his wrists, digging her nails into his flesh so hard she drew blood. "I can make you talk," she said, her voice low as if to give more weight to her threats.

Though no matter how hard she tried, he would not be intimidated by her, or by her Hunters.

Using a little of the energy he'd managed to muster, he opened his eyes and looked into hers, his holding not a single trace of fear. When he knew he'd caught her attention, he allowed another smile to form on his lips and whispered in a voice far more intimidating than hers, "Go ahead and try."

CHAPTER 46

I've heard rumours," Sam heard Jack say as she walked out of the aisles, "about Vampires being able to resurrect if you throw human blood on their ashes."

Danny cast a glance in Jamie's direction, before turning his attention back to the book he was flicking through. "Anyone up for a science experiment?"

Malachi glared at Danny. "No one is touching him,"

Sam threw her book down so hard it hit the table with a slap. With a sigh she turned to look at Jamie, who was still unconscious in his chair. She reached her hand out and placed her fingers on his neck, probing at the back where the bone had been snapped. The fracture felt almost fully healed now, the spot where it had been soft before now as solid as it should have been.

"He'll be awake soon," she said pulling out a chair and sitting down. "He shouldn't be healing as fast as he is."

Jack nodded his head. "An injury like that is supposed to

take a day to recover from. It's only been about fifty minutes."

"Anybody find anything useful yet?" she asked, looking around the table hopefully.

She was met with a chorus of unenthusiastic mumblings of 'no' and 'not yet' as well as a few dejected head shakes.

Sam sighed, closing her eyes tightly as she let out a slow breath.

"I think I might know what's wrong," Sam finally stated. Reluctantly, she pushed the record book forward and opened it to the last entry.

On the page were sketches of various symbols, scrawled in the corners and around the edges of the pages in faded brown ink.

One of them in particular she had found most interesting.

With the index finger on her left hand she pointed to it, and everyone leaned in to get a good look. Once they had all seen it, she stretched out her right arm on the table, palm facing upwards, so that they could compare the mark on the paper with the one on her wrist.

"This is a book of executions," she said. Pointing again to the symbol that was scrawled in the corner. "Apparently the first one killed in this entry was the daughter of someone repeatedly referred to as *Her*, and this mark, is apparently *Her* mark . . . whoever she is."

"That's your mark," Danny stated, his eyes glaring at the symbol on the page. "This has to be some kind of trick, because I saw you age up from baby size so I'm pretty sure you weren't burned at the stake in the past."

"No, it wasn't *me*," Sam agreed. "But I *remember* this happening."

Jade laughed. "You can't remember something you weren't there for, that's not how it works. Not unless you're psychic. Are you psychic?"

"I'm not psychic!" Sam snapped with annoyance. "But I *do* remember this . . . I've had dreams about this exact execution, so somewhere in my mind I *remember*. But that's not the point. The point is, Jamie told me that he's been having a dream, or nightmare, that's been affecting his sleep. And I believe it's the same dream, or memory, or whatever it is. And with that being my mark, I'm thinking that maybe he got the memory from my head through my blood and it's fucking him up on the inside."

Jack looked at her strangely for a moment, then let a sigh. He pulled out one of the books from the pile they had gone through and let it drop on top of the record of executions.

"This is a book on the Magic of souls and blood," he stated. "This person believes that memories are stored in two places. Within a bloodline and within a soul. If we were to work under this theory it is possible that the memories you have of this execution could come from your bloodline. So the Witch who was killed could be an ancestor of yours, or alternatively, the two of you share a soul and the memories are not yours but a residue of its past owner."

"As fascinating as all of this is," Malachi said, "it has nothing to do with our current predicament."

"Well, to be fair, I don't think we really know what the current predicament is yet," Madison said as she closed her own book.

Sam nodded towards it as Madison threw it on top of the pile. "What did you learn from that?" she asked.

Madison looked from Sam to the book, then back again and shrugged. "Nothing much. The whole thing is just the basics on Vampires. Nothing you wouldn't know already."

Sam chewed her lip for a moment as she thought. "Well, following on from blood Magic and Vampires, I have a theory," she said slowly, "and a plan that may sound really crazy once I say it all out loud . . . so everyone feel free to have better theories and plans."

"Whatever it is, I'm sure I've heard crazier," Jade said with a smile.

"Okay, well, like Jack just said Magic can be passed through bloodlines. I've always known that my Magic exists in every part of me, including my blood. Evangeline once told me that if a Vampire were to drink my blood it would be possible for them to absorb some of my Powers—"

"Yes," Malachi interrupted, with a roll of his eyes. "This is all stuff that you said earlier . . . provide some new and enlightening and *helpful* information."

"How about you shut your mouth for one second and let me get to the point of what I'm *trying* to say?"

They glared at each other for a moment, but then with a sigh Malachi eventually unfolded his arms and muttered, "Continue."

"The basics of it are what I said earlier. I think that he's absorbed my Power through consuming my blood and I think it's hurting him from the inside because he's a Vampire and not built to physically be able to contain that kind of Power.

"But, Vampires are more adaptable than most other non-humans, and I think the Magic might be able change him from the inside so that he can adapt to be a suitable host. I think it would probably have worked easier if he had taken in small doses of Magic over a long period of time. That way he could slowly adapt and build up to a stage where he can maintain a high level of Power. But he's taken it all in at once and his body isn't able to adapt as quickly as he's changing."

"Your theory does have merit," Malachi agreed thoughtfully. "When we take in new recruits we have to train them gradually so as not to overwhelm them. We tell them the training only takes about five years, but really it takes about fifty to get them to a level where they'd be considered actually powerful."

"Alright," Jade said. "So if it was your blood that made him crazy then why did it take about a week before it started affecting him like that? I don't want to poke holes in the only theory we seem to have, but if your blood was the problem wouldn't he have been evil from the moment he drank it?"

Sam let a sigh and turned to Madison. "You read the book on Vampires right? What did it say about nutrient absorption?"

Madison looked at her curiously for a moment. "What?"

"About six days," Danny replied. "That's what it said in the one I read anyway. It takes about six days to absorb all of the nutrients from the blood that's been consumed and for their bodies to flush out all of the foreign DNA."

"So, while he had my blood in his veins the Magic didn't overwhelm him."

"But once the last of your blood had been worked out of his system his body had to deal with a nutrient it wasn't used to and his body is trying to adapt as best it can," Danny continued. "Which by the looks of it, it's not doing very well."

"So that's the problem," Malachi stated, staring at Sam. "What's your solution?"

"My plan is to give him a continuous supply of my blood."

"What?" Jack gaped at her. "No . . . that *did* sound as crazy as you thought it would. There are so many things that could go wrong with that plan . . . first one, he kills you —"

"I'm not giving him *all* of my blood," Sam interrupted before he started listing off every single downside he could possibly think of. Which she was sure would be more or less the same long list of things she'd already considered. "I'm just going to give him small doses of it every day until his body is able to adapt to the Magic properly. I figure since it's my

Magic that's in his body, my blood should be able to get him to a stable place faster than anything else could.

"If anyone else has a better plan, feel free to let me know. Otherwise someone get me a needle, because I'm pretty sure he'll be awake soon."

CHAPTER 47

$\mathcal{J}$amie's eyes shot open as his head snapped to the side. He knew by the throbbing pain in his jaw that someone had punched him in the face. Slowly, he blinked his eyes and turned to find the source of his pain.

He felt his lips pull down at the corners in a scowl as he saw Danny standing in front of him with a wide grin on his face. "Morning Sunshine," he said in a mocking tone.

Jamie's lips curled back, revealing his teeth, and he let out a low growl, glaring at Danny as he did. He tried to stand, but couldn't. His body had been chained to a chair. Briefly he thought about smashing it and breaking free, smiling internally at the pain he would inflict on Danny once he'd escaped. But before he could even attempt it, Sam pushed Danny out of the way and stood in front of him.

"Okay," she said. "Turns out you're not possessed like we thought you were."

Jamie let an irritated sigh. "Then unchain me."

"I can't," she said, shaking her head. "You're not possessed but there *is* something wrong."

Jamie huffed. "There's nothing wrong with me!"

She ignored him. "I have a theory, and we should probably have a conversation about it."

Jamie looked at the faces of the people that surrounded him, before his eyes settled back on Sam's. "Fine . . . I'll talk to *you*, but only if everyone else leaves the room."

"Okay," Sam replied agreeably. She turned to everyone else expectantly.

"It's a trap!" Danny argued. "I can see it in his eyes."

Jamie smiled innocently. "What exactly do you think I'm going to do?"

"He won't hurt me," Sam said, folding her arms across her chest. "He can't kill me, and won't escape. At *most* he could use me as a hostage but I don't think he'd get very far before Jack broke his neck again."

Everyone gaped at her before Jack finally replied, "She's right." He looked at Jamie, glaring. "I know where you live, and I'll find you if you try *anything* funny."

"Right then, leave," she said, waving her hand dismissively. "It's fine."

"But . . . " Danny stared at her, clearly confused by the turn of events. But with a sigh he turned and stormed out of the room.

As Jamie watched everyone follow Danny outside, he wondered exactly where he was. It looked like a library, but not the one in town. This one was a lot larger and far grander. Curious, he allowed his eyes to wander, only turning his attention back to Sam when he heard her drag a chair forward.

"Tell me how you've been feeling," she said, watching him as carefully as he watched her.

Jamie let a sigh and allowed his body to go limp in the chair, the chains now the only thing keeping him from sliding to the floor. "I feel *fine*."

"Okay, I know you're not possessed—"

"Then unchain me," he said through his teeth.

"I'm not unchaining you because you'll just try to leave."

Jamie smiled slightly. "If you wanted to chain me up you could, at the *very* least, make it kinky."

She rolled her eyes, and tried to hide her smile. "We both know you can't handle kinky. Now tell me how you've been feeling."

"I *told* you," he said with a sly smile. "I feel kinky."

With a tired sigh she reached behind her, picking something off the table. Jamie didn't see what it was until she held it up for him to see. It was a syringe—a very large syringe—and it appeared to be filled with blood. Jamie looked at it curiously, feeling his hunger build at the sight of the crimson liquid. "What's that for?" he asked, staring transfixed at the needle.

Sam smiled. "I'm going to inject you with this. But I'm not sure what will happen because you won't answer my question. How have you been feeling?"

"Hungry," Jamie answered, not taking his eyes off the syringe. "Right now, I'm hungry."

Sam nodded. "When was the last time you fed?"

"Feels like days," he replied dozily, half zoned out.

"Jamie," Sam leaned in closer, and his focus switched to her. "I need you to *think*. When was the last time you fed?"

Jamie took a minute to think, not taking his eyes off Sam, knowing that if he saw the blood again he would become distracted. "I don't know . . . was it when we had Madison at my house?" he questioned, unable to clearly remember. "But I must not have had enough . . . I feel *starved*."

"I knew it!" Sam declared with a triumphant smile.

Jamie watched her curiously.

"Alright, when you drank my blood it pretty much fucked up your insides. You absorbed my Magic and your body isn't able to function normally right now."

He glared. "But I feel *fine.*"

"No," she replied. "You feel starved, remember? Your body is craving something, but it's not food . . . it's Magic. You need a constant supply to keep you balanced, or what you've already absorbed will burn you up from the inside.

"I'm going to inject you with this, and I'm pretty sure you'll be fine."

Jamie nodded his head slowly.

"I'm going to unchain you now. Promise you won't fight me?"

He nodded once more. "I promise."

With a click of her fingers, the chains that bound Jamie to the chair fell away and hit the floor with a crash. He attempted to stand, but Sam placed a hand on his shoulder to force him back down. "Lift up," she said, eyeing his top. "This is going straight to your heart."

CHAPTER 48

*J*amie's eyes went wide at her words and Sam could tell, by the way his eyes slowly shifted from the needle she held in her hands to the door, that he was thinking about running.

He jumped up with a superhuman speed that Sam was unable to match, and rushed past her, moving towards the door in a blur. Luckily, Sam had placed an excess amount of magical barriers on the door when everyone had left.

She was sure that while Jamie stood at the door in confusion, attempting to prise it open, everyone else was doing exactly the same on the other side.

With a sigh she got to her feet and Jamie looked over his shoulder at her. His eyes narrowing as he glared. Despite how unpredictable his moods had been lately, and despite the amount of aggression he was currently emanating, she knew that he wouldn't actually hurt her. Well . . . at the very least he wouldn't kill her.

Slowly, he turned around. Fully facing her, he leaned his back against the door and folded his arms. "You've locked me in," he stated calmly, as though it was nothing more than a simple observation.

"No," Sam said as she shook her head. "I've locked them *out.*"

He raised an eyebrow as he gazed at her assessingly.

"You wanted to be alone, right?"

The way his eyes made their way slowly down the length of her body and back up again made her insides shiver excitedly, but at the same time made her feel slightly nauseated. He wasn't being himself and Sam was unhappy because she liked him as he normally was.

A slow smile spread across his face as his eyes met with hers. "I *did* want to be alone," he breathed as he pushed himself away from the door and started moving towards her. He paused halfway between her and the door and turned a glare on the needle in her hand. Sam followed his line of sight and stared at the object she held, wondering if he would ever just get close enough so she could stab him and be done with it.

She gasped as the needle suddenly exploded in her hand, covering her palm with blood. "What the—"

"I don't need that," he said. "I'm fine."

Sam jumped slightly, surprised to find him standing right beside her.

He reached forward and dipped his finger into the blood that stained her hand and raised it to his face, examining it carefully.

"Did you—"

"It's not even human," he interrupted. Then slowly, he turned his gaze to Sam. "I doubt it would have helped, not that there's anything that *needs* help."

With a sigh, Sam shook her hand, allowing splashes of blood and glass to hit the floor. She then wiped the leftover stain on her jeans, feeling apprehensive at the idea of having to use plan B and wishing she'd thought to request a backup needle.

Or a knife.

Jamie was so close to her that she could feel the Power emanating from him.

Her Power . . . How had she not sensed it before?

The worrying part was that with Sam's Magic added to his already heightened senses, Jamie was undoubtedly stronger than her. She'd never come face to face with anyone stronger than her in Power. The Powers didn't seem to be getting weaker, but his psychological ability to handle them was. Which was *not* good. The last thing she needed was someone with ultimate Power going completely insane. The only upside, was that Jamie seemed to require a supply of energy from her in order to sustain himself.

With a sigh she rolled up her sleeve and placed her wrist before his face. He looked at it in confusion.

"Bite me," she said. "And make it quick, because the whole mind tricks won't work so it's gonna feel really weird for me."

He tilted his head to the side slightly, eyeing her wrist as though he didn't know what it was, then looked at her as if she were insane.

"You want me to bite you?"

"*Want* is a strong word."

He pushed her arm away from his face. "I don't get it. You blood tastes strange and made me feel sick last time." He raised an eyebrow. "Is this a sex thing?"

Sam rolled her eyes. "No. It is *not* a sex thing. Does this feel like a sexy situation to you?"

"Not really . . . It's why I was confused."

"You need Magic!" Sam yelled, frustrated by his severe lack of cooperation and misunderstanding of the situation, which she had already explained to him. "My Magic is in my blood, therefore you need to drink my blood!"

"Is this a test?"

"What? How—"

He moved in closer, invading her personal space so much that his face was barely an inch from hers. "Earlier you said that you didn't think I was possessed, but you're trying to trick me into drinking your blood like before, because you know I only would if I was possessed . . . Well, I'm not falling for it."

He backed away and folded his arms across his chest, smiling smugly. "You can't trick me like that, because there's nothing wrong with me and I'm not possessed."

Sam rolled her eyes and sighed, resisting the urge to punch him in the face, hold him down and force the blood down his throat.

The only reason she didn't try to forcibly make him drink was that she could feel the high levels of Power that emanated from him, and though she hated to even think it she knew that at this stage he was stronger than her.

Both physically and magically.

Although he may not necessarily know all of that, a physical altercation would be a good way for him to find out.

And for now at least—while he was still as unstable as he was—she didn't want him to know that she wasn't as strong as him.

With no other real options left, she gazed at him through half-lidded eyes and with an artful smile gracing her lips said, "Fine . . . you caught me. It's a sex thing.

Jamie cocked his head to the side as he stared at her. "You want me to bite you? *Why?*"

"I thought you said you felt kinky?"

"Well yeah, I did say that . . . "

"Unless, I was right and you *can't* handle it."

"I *can*," he declared defensively, seeming insulted by her insinuation. "Fine," he said, placing his hand on the back of her head and pulling her in closely, "if you want kinky, I will give you kinky."

Without another word, he brushed her hair away from her shoulder and bit into her neck. Without even an attempt to make it painless, his teeth pierced her skin.

Being fed on by a Vampire was not as romantic as humans seemed to believe it was. The pain of having your blood torn out of your body was excruciating to begin with and when it eventually started to subside, she was left with a hollow feeling in her stomach.

The feeling of being used in an unscrupulous manner.

It was *not* a good feeling.

It was not kinky.

It was not romantic.

But she endured it because she had to, for Jamie's sake. Though the whole time she wished she was nothing more than human and susceptible to the Vampire mind tricks that would whisper into her subconscious and convince her that this was enjoyable.

She had estimated that he wouldn't need to be injected with a lot for the Magic to help balance him out immediately, providing that it was injected directly to his heart and would be pumped through his body immediately from there.

Consuming it this way, she wasn't sure how much he would need, or how long it would take to help him.

Which was why she bit her tongue, closed her eyes and let him drink until he finally stopped.

Slowly he lifted his head from her neck and paused.

"Your holding your breath," he said quietly.

Sam nodded, letting out some air. "Yep," she said, her neck throbbing in pain where there it was now swollen and bleeding.

He moved back slightly, his hand still in her hair. Sam looked at his eyes, which were now a luminous blue reflecting newly absorbed Magic. But more importantly than that, they were filled with a look of concern. "I don't think that was a sex thing."

"What gave it away?" she asked, her voice coming out quietly, barely able to manage sarcasm with her extremely low levels of energy. "Was it the extreme lack of pleasure? Or the sheer discomfort of the entire situation?"

He put his hand to his mouth and quickly wiped away any traces of blood, staring at her in shock. "Why would you make me do that if it wasn't a sex thing?"

"Like I said," she said, placing a hand on her neck, putting pressure on the wound in an attempt to calm the pain. "You needed my Magic. My Magic is in my blood. My blood was in that syringe. And that was my only needle. Which made this my only plan B."

CHAPTER 49

*J*amie watched Sam for a few moments. Unsure of what he could say or do to make the situation better, or at the very least make her feel better.

With a sigh she swayed slightly on her feet, and he knew by the look of her that he'd taken more of her blood than he should have done. If she were human he probably would have killed her. The fact that she wasn't meant that she would survive the blood loss, but it also meant that she was not susceptible to the thought he usually sent out when feeding, the one that made humans feel at ease when being fed on.

As a Vampire, Jamie had only been fed off once before. That was by Bethany when she was on the brink of death and in need of an external energy source. The feeling of being fed on as a Vampire did not feel the same as it had when he had been human. It was painful, and caused a severe feeling of discomfort.

He could only imagine how Sam felt right now, and he felt

awful for having inflicted such negative emotions within her.

Though despite her obvious discomfort, and the fact that blood was seeping from her neck through the fingers she pressed against her wound, she smiled at him and asked, "Are you normal yet? Because I don't think I can afford any more blood loss today. And also, at the very least you owe me a cookie for that."

Jamie brought his hand to his mouth and bit down on his thumb. He reached out towards Sam. She looked at it for a moment, then moved her fingers from her neck and turned her head to the side.

With his wounded thumb, Jamie rubbed his blood on to her neck. Allowing his blood to mix with hers and healing the wound almost instantly.

"I thought *that* was the least I could do, since you seem to be unable to heal right now."

"Inside first," Sam said with a sigh, leaning back against a table to rest. "Need to restore the internal energy levels before wasting it all on a cut. And no, I still want a cookie. It's what they give you in the hospital when you donate blood."

He watched her sway, and, for the second time since he'd become conscious, remembered that he had no idea where they were.

Looking around, he eyed the multitude of tables and chairs, the shelves and the piles of books and knew they were definitely in a library of some sort, but not the one in town.

"Did we leave town?" he asked curiously, as the door behind him rattled slightly. He pointed towards it. "I think everyone wants to come back inside."

Sam shrugged. "They'll be fine. And yes we left town. This is another dimension. *The Underworld,* that's what it's called. Where the Warlocks live. This is the Archive, or that's what they called it anyway."

"Warlocks?"

Sam smiled slightly, folding her arms across her chest. "Yeah, your *brother* is apparently their new leader."

Jamie flinched at the accusation in her statement. "I didn't—"

Sam cut him off before he had a chance to defend himself. "I believe you."

He froze in surprise. "You do?"

She nodded. "I don't have a lot of friends, and I really don't want to fight with you about any more stupid things. So I'm choosing to trust you."

"Thank you . . . "

"Yeah," she shrugged, "whatever."

"I would hug you but—"

"I'd rather you didn't touch me right now."

He nodded. "That's what I thought."

"You can do me a favour and open the portal to get us the hell out of here though."

For a moment he stared at her in confusion, unsure why she had requested this of him. He wondered if she was suffering a delirium due to blood loss. He laughed. "Are you insane? I can't do that, you do it."

"You just consumed my Magic," she stated. "Until I'm fully healed, I don't have any to spare on a portal. You have lots to spare, so you'll have to make the portal."

"Why don't we let everyone in and one have of them do it?"

"Because Jack wants to stab you and if we open the door he'll just attack you, and then Danny will attack you. Malachi will attack them. And Madison and Jade will try to break it all up. And while that's happening, I'll be passed out on the floor due to having no blood, energy or Power to do anything but go unconscious. I need you to open the portal so I can go home and use a potion to heal myself."

"You could have some of my blood, if that would help?"

Sam stared at him incredulously for a moment, then sighed. "That's a stupid plan. We'll just end up spending the rest of the day trading blood back and forth, because when I take some of yours, you'll need more of mine, then I'll need more of yours and round and round we go."

Jamie ran his hand through his hair. His mind frantically trying to come up with another plan. Any other plan. One that didn't involve him having to use any form of Magic. Or have to walk through a portal.

"But what if—"

"Jamie," Sam cut him off. He looked at her, and she gazed at him, her eyes seeming very tired. "Please," she said, "I need your help. I can walk you through it."

Unable to deny her when she needed his assistance—especially when she'd never asked him for help before—he nodded, following her instructions and opening a portal to take her home.

CHAPTER 50

*J*ade's head shot up.

She had never really felt Magic before. But just then the air became permeated with a very strong, overwhelming force the likes of which she couldn't even explain with words. An undeniable force of Power, of energy that shot out from behind the locked doors of the Archives and sent shockwaves of energy that shook Jade to her very core.

And although she had never felt Magic before, she knew that that's what the feeling was.

And if she, the only non-magical person here, was able to feel the aftermath of whatever Magic Sam or Jamie were weaving in there with such force, she had no doubt that the other's must have felt it a lot stronger.

The fact that they had was evident in the way all of their heads shot up in unison, and they all looked towards the doors.

Everyone stood with their mouths parted slightly, each

looking as though they wanted to say something but did not know the words.

Jade turned her attention to Jack, who stood slightly apart from the rest, and a lot closer to the doors than any of the others dared to be. For the past fifteen minutes he'd been doing nothing but standing there, clenching and unclenching his fists, pushing and pulling at the doors, kicking at them while swearing all manner of curses, some of which Jade had never heard before, then back to clenching his fists and repeating those actions again and again.

He was the first one to regain the ability to move after the level of energy ebbed. With his jaw clenched tightly, he pulled the door by its handle. From the way he stumbled slightly when it opened, she could tell he had expected it to put up more resistance than it had.

Whatever had been blocking it before was no longer there and the door opened without protest.

Jack was the first one to storm inside, followed closely by Danny who seemed just as annoyed.

Malachi popped his head out first, looking inside, probably to see if Sam was still in there, or maybe just to assess what damage may have been done to his Archive while they'd all been locked outside. Madison sighed and walked passed him, shaking her head slightly in his direction. He stood up straight and followed her inside, though he also made a little bit of effort to walk slightly faster than her, making it appear as though she was the one following him and not the other way around.

Jade stayed by the doorway, just watching everyone and everything. As always, there was nothing much she could do to help the situation as she was only human, so she did her best to stay out of the way and let the others do their thing.

"Son of a bitch!" Jack screamed as he got to the centre of the room, where there was a small pool of blood on the floor. With a growl of anger, he spun around and kicked one of the chairs half way across the room. It hit into one of the shelves and knocked a lot of books to the floor.

"Hey!" Malachi yelled, glaring at Jack. Jade wasn't sure if he was annoyed about the broken chair, offended by the fact that technically Jack had called his mother a bitch, or concerned for his brother's well being.

Jack started to pace back and forth as he shouted things like; "I am going to *kill* that Vampire when I get my hands on him . . . I will make him sorry he ever looked in her direction! I'll burn his fucking house down while he's inside it if he even touches her! I can't believe he fucking took her!"

Jade sighed as she tried to tune out Jack's shouting. She had known Sam for a very long time and she had seen how Jamie was around her enough times that she was confident in the thought that if both of them were missing, it was more likely that Sam had been the one to coerce him into going somewhere against his will.

Because as much as Sam liked to believe that she was always a victim, Jade knew her enough to know that Sam wasn't the type to be victimised.

CHAPTER 51

*J*amie stepped through the portal with Sam in his arms. She hadn't requested that he carry her, in fact she was strongly opposed to the proposition, but after she'd attempted to stand up straight without the support of the table and promptly fell to the floor, he decided it would be best if he did. As well as that he thought that perhaps if he were to help her as much as was possible his guilt would be somewhat alleviated.

When they arrived in her living room she sighed and wriggled in his arms, attempting to push herself away and stand again, even though he was certain that if she had been unable to support her own body fifteen seconds ago she would not suddenly be able to do so now.

"It's fine," he assured, holding onto her securely. "I can carry you 'til you get your strength back."

She turned to him for a moment, the expression in her eyes somewhere between amusement and horror. It didn't take

Jamie long to realise that her horror was not at the thought of being a burden to someone, but was at the idea of having another person care for her . . . of *needing* another person to care for her.

Or perhaps she just didn't like the idea of *him* being the one to care for her. Thinking on it, he was sure that if Jack was the one carrying her she'd gladly allow it without complaint.

"I'm alright," she insisted.

Jamie refused to put her down. "Tell me where you need to go."

She rolled her eyes and sighed, reluctantly accepting the fact that she couldn't walk herself where she needed to be if she wanted to. "Just throw me on one of the chairs in the attic. I'll be fine once I get there."

Jamie carried her up the stairs, moving slowly to avoid jostling her too much, though the pace of his movements only seemed to increase her annoyance. He continued up to the attic, Sam opening the door on the way, and gently placed her on one of the wooden chairs by the table in the corner. Once seated, Sam let her body relax and she sighed, turning her head to face the shelves that lined the walls.

"What do you need me to get?" he asked.

She nodded towards the shelf that was filled with tiny glass bottles of coloured liquid. "The red one," was all she said.

Jamie stepped towards the shelves and searched for a moment, then pulled down the vial containing the red liquid as he was instructed. He gazed at it curiously as he brought it over to Sam, knowing what it was by the sight of it.

But as he handed it to her, he found himself asking, "What is it?"

She pulled the cork from the top of the vial and drank the contents, her nose crinkling as she swallowed it. "Blood," she stated, her teeth now stained.

Jamie couldn't help but gape at her. "Blood?"

She nodded as she ran her tongue across her teeth to clean away all traces. "Vampire blood," she said, as though that would offer sufficient explanation. She looked in his direction and sighed. "You're the one who asked if it would help, and now you're surprised I took some?"

"I suppose," he said as he glanced over his shoulder at the numerous red vials. "I just didn't expect you to have a supply of Vampire blood on your shelves."

"Don't worry," she said with a smile. "It's not yours. I got it at the Faerie markets. You can buy pretty much anything there. Anyway ... " she sighed and rolled her shoulders, pushing herself to her feet. Jamie rushed forward, ready to catch her if she fell.

She didn't, though she still didn't seem completely stable either. "Syringe."

"What?"

"You're going to need to take a regular dose of my blood. Injecting it would be best, but I suppose you could also mix a few drops with human blood. If you're injecting it then once every week should do it. Ingesting . . . you'll probably have to take some every day."

"I have to take your blood every day?"

Sam nodded, as though the idea didn't bother her as much as it should have.

"But . . . I don't want to drink your blood."

"You have to," she replied, looking straight into his eyes.

"Will I die if I don't?"

Sam gazed at him for a moment, then finally she sighed. "No."

"Then I won't take it."

"You *have* to."

"No, I don't. If I won't die from not taking it, then it's not necessary."

"You won't die," she stated. "You'll go insane."

"Bu—"

"Your body wasn't built to handle the kind of Power you now have, but you can adapt providing you get a regular supply. No supply, you won't adapt and the Power will tear you apart from the inside until eventually it drives you completely mad. Then you'll have Powers as strong as mine and no sanity to keep you from killing anything and everything . . . Is that what you want?"

He shook his head.

"Then I guess you'll have to get used to the idea of drinking my blood. So, would you rather inject it or consume it?"

"Injecting it would make me feel like a drug addict."

She slapped her hand down on the desk. "Consume it is then."

Sam walked past him and over to the shelves that lined the wall at his back. She knelt down and began rummaging through the boxes on the bottom shelf. Jamie turned to watch her, his mouth dry and his body extremely uncomfortable at the thought of drinking from Sam again. Especially knowing how uncomfortable it was for her.

"Sam," he said, taking a step towards her. "I can't. I can't do that to you again."

She looked up at him, her eyebrows furrowed in confusion. "Do what again?"

"I can't." He shook his head, kneeling down beside her so that they were at eye level. "I can't drink any more of your blood. I can't do that to you again."

A slow smile spread across her face, and she looked more amused than he felt she should have been. The situation they were discussing, at least as far as he was concerned, was nothing to be entertained by.

"You won't be taking anything straight from me," she said, her expression still amused. She pulled a box off the shelf and fully removed the lid so that Jamie could see inside. The box appeared to be filled with medical supplies of some kind; needles and tubes and other equipment. He wondered momentarily where Sam had obtained any of the things within the box and what exactly she needed them for, but he didn't question it aloud.

She pulled out a needle and a plastic bottle. "I'm going to put some of my blood in this," she said, waving the bottle in front of his face. "Then you're going to keep the bottle in your fridge at home, and use the needles to add two or three drops of it to the blood you usually drink. I figure this bottle should last a pretty long time if you're consuming it that way."

Jamie nodded along. He still wasn't quite on board with the idea of having to consume Sam's blood at all, but taking it in small drops from a bottle was better than the alternative.

She placed all of the medical items back in the box and sighed. "I'll have to do this in, like, an hour or something. Still not really healed enough to do it now." She closed the lid and looked up at him. "You alright?"

It took him a moment before he realised she had spoken, and when his brain did register the fact that she had asked him a question, it was one that he wasn't entirely sure how to answer.

He let a sigh and ran a hand through his hair. "I'm not sure," he said truthfully. "It's been a long, and strange, and stressful week I suppose. I feel like myself, I think. But then I think that maybe I'm not myself because I thought I was fine before and I wasn't. So, how can I really know?"

Sam nodded her head and smiled, placing a hand on his knee. "I think you'll be fine. You know what they say about people right? Only the crazy ones think they're sane. So I guess for as long as you question whether or not you're alright instead of being fully sure of it, then you must be o —"

Jamie jumped when the attic door burst open with a loud bang and Jack stormed inside.

He only had time to look in Jack's direction before a hand was twisted in the front of his top and he was pulled to his feet so harshly that he stumbled forward and almost fell flat on his face.

"What the fuck!" Sam yelled, grabbing onto Jack's arm to prise him off.

Jamie looked to Jack curiously. The man looked completely furious, his jaw clenched in anger. Without warning, the fist that wasn't holding Jamie up punched him right in the face. The hit was so hard that Jamie fell to the floor. He sat there for a moment, half in shock and half in pain.

For a Ghost, Jack could hit extremely hard. He could still feel the pressure of the punch lingering on his jaw. He placed a hand on his face and opened his mouth, moving his jaw up and down to test the level of pain and any damage there may have been.

"Get up!" Jack yelled, moving towards him. Jamie could tell by the way he moved and the way he glared, that he was looking for a fight. A fight with Jack was not something that he wanted, for a few reasons.

One of which was he liked Jack, and another was he wasn't sure that he could win.

In his peripheral he could see everyone standing in the doorway. All of them looking as stunned as Jamie was and none of them moving.

Until Jack grabbed hold of Jamie and dragged him to his feet once more.

When it looked as though Jamie was about to be punched again, Malachi shouted something that Jamie didn't hear and tried to move towards him. But he was pulled back by Madison who held him out of concern, and Danny who kept him back so that he wouldn't interrupt the beating that Jamie was obviously about to receive.

Jade just seemed to be too stunned to move as all she did was stare, mouth open in shock.

"Jack, get off him!" Sam yelled, grabbing onto Jack's shirt and using it to pull him back. She hit his arm multiple times until his grip faltered and he let Jamie go.

Jamie stood there, unmoving, unsure as to what he was supposed to do or say.

Sam pulled Jack back again, then moved so she was standing directly between them. "What the fuck is your problem?" she asked.

Jack let an irritated sigh and directed to Jamie with more aggression in his pointed finger than Jamie had ever seen before.

"*Him!* He's my problem!"

He tried to move around Sam, but she side stepped so that she remained in front of him, blocking his access to Jamie.

He huffed and leaned to the side so that he could look at Jamie as he yelled, "I liked you, you fucking dickhead! I pushed her to keep you around, to talk to you, to be your friend. And now, after all the shit you've done in the past week . . . you've made me look like a fucking idiot for liking you!"

Jamie took a step towards him. "Jack, I—"

"Shut your fucking face!" he yelled. "I don't want to hear anything from you. No more of your bullshit."

"Jack!" Sam put her hands on his chest and pushed him back slightly. Moving with him so that he was further away from Jamie. "Calm down."

"No!" He pushed Sam's hands off him. "What the hell Sam?

I mean what do you even really know about this guy? He spends the past four months around you, and in that time you get bled, Jade gets drowned, a librarian gets ritualistically slaughtered, a kid from school steals your amulet and makes people go fucking mental, and he burned half the fucking school down. Then you find out that he's fucking linked to your enemies." He gestured to Malachi, "And not even linked by profession. Linked by fucking DNA! And then when we find that out *he* goes fucking crazy and kidnaps you! Am I the only one who finds this fucking ridiculously suspicious?"

"Jack!" Sam yelled, glaring at him.

He turned his eyes to her and they stood for several seconds, glaring into each other's eyes. Seeming to communicate silently in a way that no one else could understand.

Then Sam stepped back, moving out of Jack's space. "He didn't kidnap me, I asked him to take me before you could punch him in the face. And as for the other stuff, I trust him," she said calmly. "He is one of the three people in the *entire* world that I trust with my life."

Jamie's breath caught at her words. Finding himself not only stunned and elated at her omission, but immensely proud that he—of all people—had managed to earn her trust.

Jack's shoulders slumped slightly, and he sighed. Closing his eyes for a moment. "Fine," he said to Sam. Then he walked towards Jamie, standing so close that he could feel the heat from Jack's breath as he spoke. "She trusts you, so you had better prove to me that you deserve that." He pointed a finger at Jamie's chest. "And if you do *anything* other than prove how trustworthy you are, I will kill you. I will kill you slowly and painfully. Got it?"

Slowly, Jamie nodded his head.

Jack took a step back and regarded him carefully for a

moment, arms folded across his chest. "Good." He quickly turned his attention to Malachi, who was still standing by the door, but was no longer being restrained. "You!" Malachi seemed both surprised and concerned by the fact that Jack's attention had suddenly turned in his direction. "Yeah, *you* . . . we need to have a conversation."

"About what?" Malachi asked, taking a small step back as Jack moved towards him.

Jack grabbed on to Malachi's shoulders and, without a word, teleported the both of them somewhere else.

Everyone else just looked to each other. Then Jade let a nervous laugh. "Well," she said, "that was awkward."

CHAPTER 52

Jack teleported both himself and Malachi to the middle of the woods, in one of the most isolated locations that Jack knew. As soon as their feet hit solid ground he let the Warlock go, watching with some amusement as he looked around, his face completely twisted with horror as he realised that Jack had brought him to a place where no one would hear him scream.

He took a few steps away from Jack, and held his hands out in the universal sign for 'please don't hurt me'.

"If this is about that time I tried have sex with your girlfriend—"

"I'm over that," Jack interrupted.

"Is it about the time I actually had sex with her? Because she wasn't even your girlfriend then, so that's a ridiculous thing to kill me over!"

"I'm over that too." Jack let a sigh and leaned against a tree, folding his arms across his chest. "Listen," he said.

"Is this about the time I slept with your brother?"

"What?" Jack stared at him in confusion. "Which brother? When did that happen?"

"What? Nothing happened . . . Have I told you how handsome you look for someone I thought was dead?"

Jack rolled his eyes. "Shut up you idiot. I've never liked you, but I'm not going to kill you."

Malachi visibly relaxed at his words. "Oh." He put his hands into his pockets and asked, "So, what did you want to talk about?"

"Sam doesn't know."

Malachi looked at him curiously for a moment, his eyes growing slightly larger when he seemed to realise what Jack meant. "What do you mean she doesn't know? She doesn't know you—"

"No," Jack interrupted. Unsure as to what would happen to him if someone who already knew the details of his particular situation were to describe it aloud, but not wanting to find out. "She doesn't know. For some fucked up reason I'm not allowed to talk about it."

"No allowed? Says who?"

"The hags," Jack said. "Those psychic bitches who think they run the whole world and get to fuck with people's lives. Anyway, I'm not allowed to talk about it, especially not to Sam who's not allowed to know. And since you do know, I'm warning you right now don't you dare breath a word to Sam, or Jamie, or *anyone* about what you know."

"But—"

"No!" Jack yelled, pushing himself away from the tree. "You can either keep your mouth shut, or I can permanently shut your mouth for you. Which is it going to be?"

Malachi chewed his lip for a moment, as he actually seemed to consider both options before making his choice. Jack rolled his eyes at the length of time it took him to reply, and let a heavy sigh.

"Alright," Malachi said, obviously noticing Jack's annoyance. "Fine. I'll keep my mouth shut."

CHAPTER 53

By the time Jack and Malachi reappeared, Jamie was helping Sam pack a bag with some medical necessities for the journey to his house. "What are you all doing?" Malachi asked, stepping forward and peering into the bag. He raised an eyebrow and looked to Jamie curiously.

Jamie stared at him for a moment, still having a hard time adjusting to the idea that his brother was alive and standing right beside him.

In the end he averted his gaze without answering.

"We're going to Jamie's house to fill up a bottle with my blood," Sam replied, saving him the trouble.

"We?" Malachi asked, still looking at Jamie.

"Me and Sam," he said with a sigh. Grabbing the bag and moving towards the door to the attic. Sam followed close behind him.

"And me," Jack said, blocking the doorway, his arms folded across his chest.

Jamie shrugged, moving past him.

"Seriously?" he heard Sam ask.

He didn't hear much else of whatever conversations took place. But by the time he got outside and heard the door close behind him, he looked back to find that everyone was tagging along on their little journey.

With a sigh, Jamie turned and led the way to his house.

CHAPTER 54

*J*amie chose to walk home as he had already travelled by portal more times today than he would have liked. That particular mode of transport, as convenient as it may have been, didn't feel natural to him so he didn't feel comfortable with even the idea of using one.

So he opted to walk from Sam's house to his. And since Sam was coming with him, and Jack had chosen to chaperone Sam, and Malachi had wanted to stay with Jamie, and everyone else didn't want to feel left out, they all had to walk there.

The journey was long, and most of it was in silence. Jamie had hoped to spend this time talking to Sam in an attempt to clear the air between them as he thought perhaps they should with everything that had happened between them lately.

Although, as she apparently trusted him with her life, he wasn't sure if Sam would share the opinion that the air between them needed clearing.

The thought of Sam trusting him to that extent still confused him as he wasn't entirely sure what exactly he had done to earn her trust to that magnitude. Especially considering how he'd behaved towards her over the past week. Somewhere in the back of his mind he thought that the words had been something she'd spoken without real meaning just to get Jack to back off and cease his attempt to beat him to death.

But then there was the other part of him that was elated at the idea that she did trust him to the extent that she'd claimed.

The whole idea of it was causing him more stress than it should have and he felt that if he could just talk about it in depth with Sam it would help calm his mind. But of course, that was not a subject he felt comfortable discussing with an audience.

It was completely dark by the time they got to his house, darker than it should have been due to the thick canopy of trees. Jamie walked to the door first, with Sam, Danny and Jack the only ones who were able to follow as they were the only ones who had previously been invited past the runes that protected the area surrounding his home.

Jade, who had never set foot inside his home was among those stuck at the tree line.

The last time Madison was at Jamie's house he'd been forced in by those permitted entry, dragged inside against her will and had never actually been *invited*.

And Malachi . . . well, of course *he'd* never been inside as they thought each other dead only hours ago.

Jamie looked over his shoulder to Jade, Madison and Malachi and said, "Come on."

They all looked around nervously for a moment before continuing on and following Jamie into his house.

The chair they'd had Madison tied to earlier was still in his living room, a bundle of ropes on the floor beside it.

"Ah, memories," Madison sighed as she stepped in to the house behind him, gazing over his shoulder at the chair.

Sam walked straight through the living room and into the kitchen. Jamie followed her, grabbing hold of the chair on his way past and returning it to its rightful place in the corner of the room.

The kitchen was a place he didn't generally bother spending much of his time. This was made obvious by the fact that the only working appliances were the fridge, the kettle and the microwave. The oven — which was blocked by storage boxes filled with games, books and DVDs that he hadn't bothered to store yet — had been neglected since the moment he'd acquired the home.

The room was not filled with grime or mould or anything that looked nearly that bad, but its neglect was obvious by the clutter of objects that didn't belong. Sam had never seen this room before, so she'd never had an opportunity to look around. But she was looking around now, and Jamie suddenly felt embarrassed that she was seeing the mess he kept his home in.

He was also very aware of the fact that he had no cutlery, no dishes apart from a few mugs, nothing in the fridge except for bottles filled with blood, and a kitchen tap that no longer provided clean drinking water because it had broken over a decade ago and he didn't use it enough to care to fix the pipe.

All of these things made him feel self-conscious at having Sam in there, though she didn't seem to care as she moved across the floor without passing comment on their surroundings.

Jamie watched as she stopped on the far side of the kitchen and began rifling through the drawers. Alarmed at the level of comfort she seemed to feel going through his things without first asking, he instinctively jumped in front of her to stop her from looking through his stuff.

As he slammed the drawer shut, Sam pulled her hands back to avoid them being hurt. She raised an eyebrow and looked to him with some amusement. "Really?" she asked. "What the hell could you be hiding in there that I'm not allowed to see?"

It was more than likely that there was nothing of particular interest within any of the drawers or cupboards, however, that did not mean he was on board with the idea or the reality of someone going through each little hideaway within his home to see what was inside.

Jamie looked down at his hand, firmly holding the drawer in place, then turned his attention to Sam and shrugged. "I have no idea what's in here," he answered honestly. "But I'm not alright with you just going through my things. Tell me what you're looking for and I'll tell you where to find it."

Sam's lips quirked in a momentary smile. She placed both of her hands on her hips and looked at him. "All I heard you say was, I don't remember where I left my porn so don't look anywhere."

Jamie stared at her for a moment, his mind suddenly thrust back to the very first conversation they had ever had. "What is your obsession with porn?"

Sam tutted a little and shook her head at him. "Just so you know, I'm judging you more for the lies."

"It's not—never mind," Jamie cut himself off when Sam moved down a bit and opened a cupboard. He moved with her and closed it before she had even managed to open it all the way. He stood in front of it, using his body to block her access to the handle.

"I need a knife!" she yelled while laughing. "I don't care about your porn!"

The door to the kitchen opened almost instantaneously after Sam had shouted. Jamie turned to find Malachi standing in the doorway. He looked at them curiously, his expression showing clear signs of amusement. "What kind of porn?" he asked.

"Get out!" Jamie ordered, pointing towards the living room.

Madison pushed past Malachi and held a dagger out to Sam. "You left this on the couch earlier."

Sam moved forward and took the blade from Madison, her eyes steely. "Thanks," she mumbled as she sat herself down on one of the kitchen chairs.

Madison smiled and walked back to the living room where the others were still waiting patiently for Sam to do whatever she needed to do.

"Seriously though, what kind?"

"Out!" Jamie ordered once more. Moving across the narrow space to physically remove Malachi from the room, who smiled as Jamie's hands made contact with his shoulders.

"I'm just trying to get to know my brother. Is that so wrong?"

Jamie gave him a final shove and slammed the kitchen door in his face. Rolling his eyes at the wood before he turned back to Sam.

"So . . . what's your stock like at the moment?"

"My stock?" Jamie asked curiously as he pushed away from the door and looked towards Sam. She was still seated on the kitchen chair, her elbows resting on the table, the handle of the blade held loosely between a finger and thumb.

"Yeah," she replied. "Food stock. How much have you got at the moment?"

"Why?" he asked, sitting down on a chair across from her, unable to hide the discomfort he felt at answering those kind of questions.

Not that Sam ever seemed to care about his answers one way or the other.

She let a sigh as she seemed to sense his reluctance to speak. "I need to know what you have right now so that I know how much I need to bleed. So, ballpark, what's it like? How many litres?"

Jamie shrugged and stood, walking over to the fridge, opening the door and peering inside. His *stock* was pretty full at the moment, as was his fridge. About 50 bottles stacked inside, each containing one litre. "Um . . ." He hesitated in his response. There was no way that Sam could afford to lose enough blood to match his current stock. He took a moment to think of what he should tell Sam.

Though he never got a chance to speak as Sam leaned across the table and peered past Jamie and into the fridge. "Wow . . . that's like seven peoples' worth," she said with a laugh. "Are you stocking up for the winter or something?"

Jamie closed the fridge door and turned, leaning his back against it. He chewed his lip and ran a hand through his hair. "I don't think this is a good idea."

Sam let a sigh and rolled her eyes. "We've already had this conversation."

"But . . . I don't feel right taking your blood. As well as that it—"

"It's only one drop per litre," Sam interrupted.

Jamie looked at her curiously.

"All it takes is one drop for every litre. My blood is where my Magic is. One drop of it mixed with human blood should be enough to transfer the Magic over. Once the blood has Magic it should keep you sane if you have one a day."

"Are you sure that's all?"

Sam nodded, then asked. "So how much right now?"

"Fifty-three."

"Okay, do you have a glass or a cup or a bowl or something? Something wider at the top than the bottle I brought. I'll let you look since I'm not allowed to touch any of your things in case I find your secrets."

"I don't have any secrets," Jamie said with a smile, striding away from the fridge so that he could look through the cupboards for one of the mugs he knew was lurking about somewhere inside.

"Mmhm . . . " Sam muttered with a dubious expression on her face. "Everyone has secrets . . . even you. In fact I heard a rumour the other day that you had a secret door to a secret basement that's filled with *your* secrets."

Without speaking another word, Jamie retrieved one of the cups from the back of the cupboard above the sink, bringing it over to the table and placing it before Sam.

She took the cup by the handle and moved it slightly, repositioning it in a way that seemed to make more sense to Sam than it would to anyone else. Then, without so much as flinching, she took the blade to her wrist and sliced the skin open.

The blood began to flow almost immediately, and Sam held her arm over the cup, allowing the drops to fall.

Jamie could do nothing but stare.

CHAPTER 55

$\mathcal{S}$am let a sigh and placed her head on the table, resting her forehead just on the edge while still holding her arm above the cup.

Jamie peered inside.

The blood dripped from Sam's wrist in a slow and steady stream so it was taking a while for the cup to fill.

In the past minute it had filled with just under one inch of blood. Not that he thought they would really need to fill the cup, completely if one drop per litre was all they needed.

Jamie jumped slightly, his attention pulled away from the sight of Sam's blood, at the muffled sounds of music.

Sam let another sigh and sat upright, rolling her eyes as she pulled a phone from the pocket of her jeans.

"I thought you broke your phone," Jamie said as she placed it on the table and held down the flashing green symbol to answer it.

"I got a new one . . . obviously."

Before Jamie had a chance to retort a voice began to speak from the other end of the phone.

"Sam?"

"What's up?" Sam asked, leaning forward slightly to look into the cup. Probably to determine how much longer she would need to keep her arm hovering above it.

Jamie looked down at the screen on the table, clenching his jaw when he saw the name of the caller.

Vicki.

He huffed and slouched back in his chair, folding his arms across his chest as he glared in Sam's direction. Silently judging her for partaking in conversation with a Vampire he saw as an enemy.

She just rolled her eyes at him.

"Um . . . have you seen Aleczander today?"

Sam furrowed her brow and looked at the phone in confusion. "No. Why would I have seen Aleczander?"

"Well . . . he left a little over two hours ago, on his own. And, well, it's been a while now and he's not been home yet. He's never out alone for this long. And some of us are starting to worry because he said he'd send word if he wouldn't be back within an hour. But he didn't."

"Where did he go?" Jamie asked.

"Who's that?" Victoria asked.

"Jamie," Sam replied. Turning her arm so that her wrist was facing the ceiling, no longer allowing the blood to drip.

"So . . . you haven't seen him either?"

Jamie could hear the concern growing in Victoria's voice the more they spoke. Remembering how small she was, and imagining the concern he heard showing on her features he, couldn't help but feel sorry for her.

And he immediately hated himself for feeling anything for *her.*

"Why would Jamie have seen him?"

"Because he went to meet with him."

"What?" Jamie asked, staring at the phone as if by doing so he could communicate the confusion in his expression to the person on the other end.

"Well, you sent him a message, asking him to meet you urgently, didn't you?"

"Jamie's phone is broken," Sam replied, looking to Jamie curiously as she spoke. "And we've been together all day. Neither of us have seen Aleczander."

"But where else would he go?" The girl's voice was beginning to sound hysterical.

"Give me a second. I'll call you back."

"Wait—"

"I'll call you back, I promise."

Sam hung up the phone. Without uttering a word she picked the knife up from the table with one hand and grabbed Jamie's arm with the other. Using the blade she cut across his hand, slicing into the palm deep enough to draw blood. Jamie cried out slightly, more from the shock than the pain.

Though he quickly silenced himself when Sam placed his hand on her wrist and he realised that Sam was just borrowing some of his blood to help heal her wounds. Though it would have been courteous of her to at least ask before just cutting him.

She stood and picked the cup up off the table, bringing it to the fridge where she placed it inside.

"You can pour that into the other bottle later. It should keep okay in there anyway. One drop with every litre," she said as she closed the door. "Try not to forget."

"I won't forget."

"Where do you think he is?" she asked, leaning her back against the fridge and gazing at him. Her mouth set in a firm line, her brows pinched together slightly in thought. "He never goes out of the dimension alone, or at all if he can help it. He'd only go if it was some kind of emergency, but if it was a big one he'd have told everyone what it was so they could prepare. He told everyone he was coming to meet you. That you sent him a message?"

Jamie shrugged. "I never sent him a message."

Sam half smiled. "Well you obviously couldn't have, your phone is —"

"I got a new one the other day," he interrupted her. "But I didn't text him."

Sam stared at him for a moment, them swiftly turned her attention in the direction of the kitchen door. "Did you have Aleczander's number in your phone?"

Jamie nodded. "Yes. I have his number and yours saved to it."

"Uh huh . . . and do you have your phone right now?"

"Um . . . " Jamie patted down the pockets of his jacket, then the pockets of his trousers.

Finding no evidence of the phone in either place he shook his head.

Sam swore under her breath and moved quickly from the kitchen. Jamie jumped to his feet to follow her. Everyone was seated on the sofa and looked as though they had been having some form of conversation before he and Sam entered the room. On their arrival the others seemed to notice there was something not quite right as the room fell suddenly silent and everyone gazed worriedly in their direction.

Sam didn't stop moving to explain what was happening or what exactly she was thinking.

It was only when she turned towards the stairs and began rushing up that Jamie realised the same thing that she must have.

If he didn't have his phone with him, then he must have left it here.

The only other person who would have access to it was Bethany.

Bethany, who surely should have woke to the sounds of seven people moving around and talking, but hadn't made an appearance.

It was only then that Jamie even thought to check if she was still inside the house.

And it was only when he did that he found she was gone.

CHAPTER 56

$\mathcal{D}$anny and Jack jumped to their feet when they heard Sam swear loudly from upstairs. Everyone else just turned their heads in the direction of the stairs.

All at once they asked what was going on.

Jamie let a sigh and answered without turning away from the stairs. "Sam got a call. Aleczander is missing. Everyone thinks he came to see me. He didn't come to see me. I never texted him, my phone was here. Bethany is gone. My phone is gone."

"Who's Bethany?" Jade asked, sounding extremely confused.

"Is she the wife?" Jack asked.

"Are you serious?" Danny yelled. "I thought you were joking earlier! When the fuck—"

"Shut up Danny," Sam spat as she ran down the stairs. "We're having a bit of a crisis right now and need to get some priorities."

"Wait . . . Bethany . . . "

Jamie turned to look at Malachi, who was watching him, his brow furrowed in concentration. "Brunette, this high?" He brought his hand up to the height of his shoulder, "Brown eyes? Absolute mental?"

"Mental? Why would you say that?" Jamie asked, unable to help his surprise that Malachi knew Bethany and wondering in what way exactly their paths had crossed.

"Oh . . . " he laughed humourlessly, nodding his head. "Trust me, she's mental. You'd have to be to do what she's done. What I'm most confused about is why you thought it was a good idea to get involved with her and also why you thought it was a better idea to marry her? Are *you* mental? Because that's insane."

"*Oh . . . *" Madison nodded along as if every mystery in the world now made sense to her. "She's the *Vampire* Vampire Hunter!" Madison swiftly turned her head in Jamie's direction, frowning at him slightly. "That is crazy . . . Did you marry her *before* or *after* you were Turned?"

Malachi moved forward and placed his hands on Jamie's shoulders, looking him directly in the eyes. "Is this a cry for help? Is that what's happening here? Is it because I left and this is a cry for help?"

Jamie brushed his hands off and took a step back. "Get off me. What are you even talking about?"

"Bethany, *your wife*, is a Vampire Hunter, who is so fucking mental she allowed herself to be Turned into a Vampire just to get an upper hand in battle . . . then proceeded to take over the operation and now leads the Vampire Hunters from behind the scenes."

Jamie stared at Malachi, completely dumbstruck, then began to laugh uncontrollably. "You're joking, right? This is a joke?"

"I *knew* she was up to something evil!" Sam yelled, apparently having no trouble believing the story Malachi had just weaved. "I *knew* it!"

Jamie just shook his head and continued to laugh. "No . . . you don't understand. Not to speak ill of anyone, but Bethany is . . . well, she's just . . . I mean there is *no way* she could orchestrate anything like what you've described. She couldn't, she's not that clever. I mean, I was there when she was Turned and she didn't do it on purpose—"

"Oh my Gods," Malachi sighed dramatically and placed a hand to his head. "It was you. You Turned her, didn't you?"

"She was dying, it's not like I planned it in advance. And there's no way she could ha—"

"Couldn't she have?" Malachi asked with a smug smile. *"Couldn't she?"*

"Did you ever tell her about your Sire?" Sam asked.

Jamie looked to her, unsure as to what that would have to do with anything. "I just told her what I knew at the time. Which wasn't a lot . . . Just a name and a face."

"You told her how you were Turned?" Sam asked. "About the girl who took you from home?"

Jamie nodded.

"Do you think that would have been enough for her to identify him?" Danny asked.

Sam let a sigh and folded her arms across her chest. "Aleczander's name and description paired with a name and description of Victoria is pretty much all it would take."

"So Aleczander Turned you?" Malachi asked, watching Jamie curiously. " . . . Interesting."

"Why would she want Aleczander?" Jamie looked to Sam as he spoke, clearly there was something he was missing. "I don't understand."

"You Turned her," Malachi explained, leaning against the

back of the sofa. "That places her in line for the throne. The previous ruler was Aleczander's mother, when she died it went to her first fledgling, which just so happened to be her son—that's how it works. So Aleczander was king. If he should die it goes to his first fledgling ... *you*. If you die, it goes to your first fledgling ... " Malachi directed his hands in Jamie's direction, pausing to allow him to guess who the throne would fall to if he were to die.

"But ... I refused to align with Aleczander, so shouldn't that take me and any of mine out of the equation altogether?"

Sam shook her head. "No. If he dies it's offered to you, whether you pledged allegiance or not. It's yours next. The only way around it is to refuse the throne if it's offered. Then it goes to Eva as Aleczander's second fledgling. Only if you refuse does it move from your line to the second. Though if you die before you get to refuse, then it's Bethany's."

For a few moments he didn't speak, needing a minute to take in the information he'd been given. He hadn't known that Aleczander was a king of anything until recently, so surely there was no way Bethany could have known any of this at the time.

There was just no way.

Even though they hadn't spent more than a few months in each others' company he'd always believed he'd known her quite well.

Well enough to find it incredibly difficult to imagine her capable of a deception on this level.

But if what Malachi was saying was true, and Bethany had been a Vampire Hunter prior to becoming a Vampire, then perhaps it would be plausible for her to know more about Vampires and the laws of their society than he would have at the time.

Did that mean their entire relationship had been one big

deception?

That idea just didn't mesh with his memories at all.

Perhaps she'd found out later . . . after they had parted ways.

"She said she'd found me," he said. "When she showed up here a few days ago, she said she'd found me. That means she'd been looking for me."

Sam shook her head. "I warned you she was up to something."

"Yeah, well you didn't know her."

She smiled slightly. "Clearly, neither did you."

"What exactly are we supposed to do?" Madison asked. "I mean, would she really take Aleczander? Would she be able to?"

Jack folded his arms across his chest and leaned against the wall by the door. "I've heard rumours, that the Vampire ruler has special powers . . . the kind that no other Vampire has."

Danny stared at Jack for a moment. "Where do you hear all of these Vampire rumours? That's the second one you've mentioned today."

Jack shrugged and smiled. "I just hear things. But if it's true, I don't think that Aleczander is in any trouble."

"We still have to do something," Sam said with a sigh. "Vicki was really upset on the phone. No one has been able to get through to Aleczander, so we need to find him."

"What kind of phone do you have?" Jade asked. It was only when everyone looked to him expectantly that Jamie realised the question was aimed at him.

"What does it matter what kind of phone he has?" Malachi asked. "I think you missed the point of the situation."

Jade rolled her eyes. "If it was a smart phone you should be able to track the GPS to find out where it is right now. If the Vampire Hunter took it, it'll tell you where she is. If she took

Aleczander it will also tell you where he is."

"It is a smart phone."

"Do you have an account set up on it or something?"

Malachi laughed. "He's not going to have anything like —"

"It's set up through Google."

Malachi gaped at him for a moment. "Google, really? Why would you even?"

Jamie shrugged. "I use it for games, books, music, films and stuff. Why, what do you do with your phone?"

"I use it for the purpose it was built for . . . calling people."

Jade laughed. "That's what elderly people who don't understand technology use phones for."

Malachi scoffed. "He's only *five* years younger than me!"

Jade pulled her phone out of her pocket. "I have an app that can track your phone." She unlocked the screen and handed the phone to Jamie. "All you have to do is sign in."

Jamie took it from Jade and followed her instructions.

Malachi snorted. "Just use a tracking spell, like a normal person."

Sam sat down on the sofa next to Jade. "Fine," she said. "You go gather the ingredients for a tracking spell, then mix the potion and cast it, while we try this and we'll have a race to see who finds Bethany faster."

"You really think she'd still have the phone on her?" Danny asked.

Jamie nodded his head. "I may not know her as well as I thought, but I really don't think she'd be smart enough to throw it away."

Jade leaned in closer, looking over at the screen on her phone. "Okay, so just give it a sec and it will tell you your phone's last known location. If it's still on, it will show you where it is now. If it's turned off it will show you the last place it was."

Jamie nodded his head, waiting impatiently for the map to continue loading.

The phone buzzed and dinged twice. Jade took the phone out of his hand and looked at the map which now depicted a vast block of green with no words displayed.

"They're in the woods," Jamie muttered.

Danny sighed loudly and sat back in his seat. "It could take us days to find them in the woods."

"Tracking spell . . . " Malachi muttered.

Jade tutted and copied the location information from the GPS app and pasted it into Google Maps. Searching directions from their current location to the location of his phone.

As most of the woods in the area were not mapped the device provided a route close to the hiking trails that were stored in its database, which gave Jamie a pretty good idea as to where they needed to go.

"Thirty-five minutes," Jade said, pushing herself to her feet. "Add an extra five or ten for the part that's not mapped."

Sam let a sigh and stood too. "That's not too bad I guess."

Jack smiled and leered superiorly at Malachi. "And *you* wanted to waste time with a tracking spell."

CHAPTER 57

Aleczander was unsure how much time had passed, but he had spent most of it feigning unconsciousness. Not allowing himself to react or to fight back even as his captors tortured him in the most unimaginative of ways to attempt to prise from him the answers to their questions.

Through all of the slicing and stabbing he did nothing but bite his tongue and remain silent. Keeping his body still until the tranquiliser they used had completely evaporated from his system.

Because he had maintained his appearance of semi-consciousness the Vampire Hunters were not aware that he was now well enough to flee if he wanted to.

Without too much probing he could sense that the two males were protected by Magic — the amulets that adorned the necks of all Vampire Hunters — so it would do no good to attempt to manipulate them into freeing him.

However, as a Vampire, the woman appeared to share the

belief that all Vampires had. The belief that their wills were so strong they could not possibly be manipulated in the same way that a human could.

"This is useless," one of the men growled. This wasn't the first time he had expressed impatience over the futility of their efforts.

The woman sighed. Aleczander could sense her frustration, her ire further aggravated by both his refusal to cooperate and her cohorts doubting her efforts.

It was because of this lack of control over her emotions that Aleczander managed to gain entry to her mind with very little effort.

Aleczander rarely made use of the extra powers that his position granted him. However, there were certain situations where being able to sway the minds of other Vampires was a skill that came in quite useful.

Situations such as this one.

Once he had latched on to the frustration that he knew Bethany was feeling he began to whisper within her mind. Murmuring words that would only serve to increase the anger and feed upon the seeds of aggression that were planted within those thoughts. As the other Vampire Hunters continued to discuss the pointlessness of their assignment and of how they should just dispose of Aleczander and get it over and done with he sensed his efforts begin to bear fruit.

Their conversations only served to add fuel to the already fast growing fire of fury that Aleczander was stirring within Bethany.

And within minutes she snapped.

Aleczander heard a metallic scraping, followed by a frustrated scream. He opened his eyes just in time to see the Vampire Hunters decapitated with just one swing of a sword. Their bodies and heads both fell to the floor with heavy thuds.

Bethany was baring her teeth at them and breathing heavily, the sword still clutched in both hands.

"Now drop the weapon," Aleczander said.

Bethany released the sword immediately. It hit the floor with a clang.

Once she was unarmed, Bethany seemed to regain some grasp over her own mind and gazed down at the bodies of her comrades, her mouth open in shock.

Then slowly she turned her head in Aleczander's direction. "What did you do to me?"

He didn't answer her question with words, instead bade her to act out more of his commands, sure that she would eventually grasp what had been done.

"Come here and untie me."

Without another word she, did so.

Once his restraints were loosened he freed his arms, stretching so as to rid himself of the aches in his shoulders.

Bethany stood quickly, acting before he had a chance to control her again, but it seemed she was unsure what to do. Before either of them could decide however, the door burst open so suddenly they both jumped in fright. Aleczander was distracted for barely a second, but it was long enough for Bethany to make her escape out of the window to the back of the room. As glass shattered the newcomers stepped inside and Aleczander recognised the swish of golden hair.

"She's getting away!" Sam shouted looking over her shoulder as she walked further into the tiny cabin. Behind her he saw Jamie turn, presumably to give chase to Bethany.

Aleczander let a sigh and stood, shaking his head. "What are you doing here?"

"I got a call to go rescue a damsel."

He laughed. "Well it looks as though the damsel has rescued himself."

"Victoria will be thrilled."

She led the way out of the cabin. Outside Aleczander was greeted by quite a few faces. Some familiar and some not. Jack and Malachi, both of whom he knew though not very well, and two girls whom he had never met.

"Glad to see you're not dead," Jack said with a smile, then turned to Sam. "Danny followed Jamie to chase down whatserface."

"There is not much point," Aleczander said. "She's already run extremely far and besides, after she killed two of her own, she is not going to find any refuge with the other Vampire Hunters."

"She killed two of her own?" the dark-skinned girl asked.

"Yeah," Sam muttered, shaking her head. "You do *not* wanna look in there."

CHAPTER 58

*J*amie chased Bethany's scent to the other side of the woods.

He knew that Danny had followed him and attempted — but failed — to keep up, but he was so far ahead of him now that his presence was barely even a blip on his radar.

Bethany, however, he could still sense ahead of him.

Moving as fast as her legs could carry her, running as though her life depended on it. Which at this stage . . . after kidnapping the Vampire King it was likely her life *did* depend on it.

Not that he would be the one to end her, he would just be the one to catch her.

At least he thought he would be the one to catch her, but after barely five minutes of chasing he felt Sam speak within his mind. Telling him to turn back, that there was no longer any point or any interest in pursuing her.

Which he believed she must have said at Aleczander's

behest as he was really the only one of them with any *real* desire to capture Bethany.

With an obedient but defeated sigh he turned back and ran towards the cabin they had found Aleczander in. On the way he ran into Danny, and slowed down his pace to match that of the Witch. Speaking to him as he passed in the opposite direction. "Sam said to turn back."

Danny let an audible sigh of irritation and turned back, running with Jamie to where the group were waiting on them.

Danny spread his arms wide and looked directly to Sam. "What the hell? I thought she was the bad guy!"

Sam just shrugged and said, "Whatever."

Aleczander smiled at Jamie when he approached. Although his clothes were torn and stained with both dirt and blood, his skin appeared completely unscathed which Jamie assumed meant that he was fine. "Thank you all for coming to my rescue," Aleczander said, looking around to everyone. "Samantha, I believe this means I owe you a favour."

"Well, technically you saved yourself just before we got there, so I guess we're cool."

He smiled and placed his hand on her shoulder. "No, it's the effort that matters. You and your friends were willing to come to my rescue when asked. So I hereby give you my oath, if you ever find yourself needing rescuing feel free to call on me and my fri—"

CHAPTER 59

amie had to blink several times to clear his eyes of the glittering lights that blinded him. Slowly, his vision began to refocus and he found that he was standing in a very large room. The floor was made of what appeared to be white marble, and the ceiling of blue crystal. The room was circular, and bordered by archways separated by Grecian pillars. Beyond the archways there appeared to be nothing but a clear nights' sky filled with stars.

From the sudden change of scenery, Jamie surmised that they had all been transported somewhere. Everyone but Aleczander was there, and he immediately worried that perhaps something nefarious had happened to him. But then he heard a beep and looked to Sam who was staring at the screen of her phone.

"Aleczander is still in the woods," she said. Clearly the same worry that had passed through Jamie's head had gone through hers. She sighed and put the phone into the pocket of her jeans. "He's alright. Heading home now."

"Where are we?" Jade asked. She was the only one who took a step away from the group and hesitantly made her way towards one of the archways across the room.

Both Danny and Malachi reached out to pull her back. Danny was the first to take hold of her by the arm. "We should all stick together," he said.

"We're in a dimension just outside of Athens," Jack replied. Jamie looked to him, noticing that he was the only one not dazed or confused by their sudden teleportation. He sighed and folded his arms across his chest. "Fair warning is always nice, but they have less manners than wild animals."

"Who?" Jamie asked curiously.

Jack smiled and indicated with his head towards the far end of the room, where there were few short steps that led up to a dais between two of the pillars, upon which was an altar, and what appeared to be the silhouettes of three women.

"The hags," Jack explained, stepping towards them.

Jamie and Sam shared a look of confusion, before Sam shrugged and began to follow Jack.

For a moment Jamie just stood back with everyone else, his mind wary and far less trusting.

The suddenness of their transportation.

The fact that they had all been brought to a strange place by people they had never met.

The fact that Aleczander had been left behind.

There was a lot about the current situation that felt off, all of which gave Jamie pause.

Slowly the others began to walk after Sam and Jack, and, unsure of what else he could do at this point, Jamie followed them as well.

They walked across the room and up the staircase to the platform where the women sat cross-legged on the floor facing them. None of them spoke or moved as they approached.

They just sat there, patiently waiting.

It was only when Sam reached the top of the stairs that they looked up at her and smiled.

Jamie shivered at the sight of them.

All three women moved in complete unison, as though they were three bodies for the same mind. It was extremely disturbing to witness.

It looked unnatural.

Jack clapped him on the back. "I get that too," he said. "They're creepy fuckers, these hags."

Jamie looked to the women once more. Unsure as to why Jack referred to them as hags. All three of them looked young enough, as though they were in their mid-to-late twenties, with features quite fair and eyes that seemed as though they could look right into a person's soul. Even with the undeniable *other* of their appearance, they were all extremely beautiful women.

There was nothing about their appearance that would warrant the word 'hags' as a descriptor.

As he mused, the women indicated for them to sit.

Sam did as requested, sitting cross-legged in front of them. Once Sam had sat down with seemingly no issue the others followed suit, though they appeared uneasy doing so.

Jamie however, did not sit. He stayed standing, his arms folded across his chest.

This only served to draw the women's attention to him.

"Please be seated," said the one in the centre of the trio.

Jamie looked at her for a moment, attempting to gauge what it was about them that felt so *wrong*. Although, when he tried to probe within her mind, he found himself blocked. The walls around her thoughts were ten times stronger than the ones blocking Sam's.

"No," he responded. "I'd rather stand."

Sam looked to him over her shoulder and rolled her eyes. "Just sit down, don't be so difficult. They're the Fates. They can't interfere. They couldn't do anything to you even if they wanted to."

"If they can't interfere then why did they?"

Sam sighed loudly. "How did they interfere?"

"They brought us here." He looked from Sam to the Fates, then back again. "They took us out of a situation, out of a conversation, to bring us here. I would say that's interfering."

Jack stood and walked back slightly, so he and Jamie were standing shoulder to shoulder. He folded his arms across his chest too. "I would agree, that does sound an awful lot like interfering."

"Silence Hunter," the woman on the left snapped. "I grow weary of your rebelliousness."

"Anything to piss you off Lachesis!" Jack yelled. "Don't start a fight with me because I'm pretty fucking sure I'm more sick of you than you are of me!"

"Okay!" Sam yelled. "Can everyone just shut the hell up? I always knew that one day I would be called here, so can we all just sit down and talk this shit out so that we can leave?"

"No." Jamie shook his head, leaning so that he was closer to Sam's eye level. "Sam, I need you to trust me. I have a really bad feeling about this—"

"It's *fine*," she argued.

"Why didn't they bring Aleczander?" Jamie asked.

Sam looked surprised by his question. "What?"

"Well look around. They didn't bring just you, they brought everyone who was with you at the time, except Aleczander."

"It was imperative that we see Samantha now," Lachesis answered.

"Alright. So you needed to see Sam now, so you pulled her here. Why did you bring the rest of us too?"

"Teleportation spells are tricky," Sam answered. "It's hard to take just one person so usually you take a radius and anyone inside it gets pulled through."

"Fine . . . Except Aleczander was standing in between us, so he should have been brought here too."

"He has a point," Malachi agreed, looking to the Fates then to Jamie. "If it was a teleportation spell, Aleczander should definitely have been brought with us if we were all pulled through."

"You were of importance, the Vampire was not," the woman on the right replied.

"Why?" Sam asked, her expression at last as wary as the others. "Why are they important and Aleczander isn't?"

"The Vampire is nothing, his neutrality determines that he can offer nothing to your future."

"Sam?" she turned to look at him. "How important is Aleczander?"

"The Vampire is not important," the Fate repeated.

"How important is he to *you*."

Sam shrugged. "I dunno . . . he's like family. But like they said he's neutral so he doesn't really come in handy in a fight."

"Have you ever asked him to fight?" Jack asked, speaking his question as though he already knew that the answer would be no.

Jade leaned forward so that Sam would be able to see her past Malachi. "But didn't he literally just make an oath to come—"

"No!" the Fate in the centre of the trio slammed her fist down on the tiled floor, which cracked slightly upon impact. She let a heavy sigh and looked at each of the group in turn.

"Everyone, be silent."

"So that's what it is then . . . " Jack said with an insolent smile. "You want to keep Aleczander uninvolved. Are you three up to no good again?"

Lachesis smiled slightly, her gaze averted down. "Hunter," she said. "I will take great pleasure in punishing you if you do not do as my sister commands and be silent."

Jack began shouting an immense amount of profanities at Lachesis who returned his words with equal passion.

While their arguing continued Jamie noticed movement out of the corner of his eye and turned swiftly only to find that there was nothing there.

Just the flame of the candles flickering in the breeze from outside.

He looked beyond the flames, to the clear sky where all looked too still to cause the flames to flicker.

He looked again, and that was when he noticed how dark the room had become in the past few minutes.

The feeling of dread began to intensify within his core and his senses urged him to flee. Every part of him could sense that there was something *very* wrong here.

"We need to leave," he said, turning to Sam. His voice must have sounded urgent as Malachi jumped to his feet without requesting any further explanation. Madison did so too, apparently willing to follow whatever Malachi did. And with so many of them standing, Jade and Danny got to their feet.

Sam remained seated for a moment longer and looked to him as if gauging his expression.

Then slowly she stood.

She sighed and turned to the Fates. "We're going."

Sam grabbed onto Jack by the arm and began pulling him away from Lachesis, whom he was glaring at as though he could make her head explode if he did it for long enough.

They had made it just a few steps when the flames on the candles extinguished and plunged the entire room into darkness.

"Sam, light!" Jamie shouted, his senses overwhelmed by a fear of the darkness he had not experienced since he was a child.

Barely a second passed before the room became illuminated in the purple glow of Sam's Magic.

Though a second seemed to be all it took, as when the room was illuminated once more every part of it seemed to be tainted by the darkness of Shadows seeping from the walls, the ceiling, the floors.

Stretching out from every surface to fill the room.

"Go!" Sam shoved him on the back, urging him to move forward swiftly. "Everyone run, get out of here."

"No!" one of the Fates screamed after them. "Keep them here, they cannot leave!"

Jamie's legs urged him to run as fast as he could, but loyalty kept him moving at the same speed as everyone else, knowing that if he made it out when no one else did he would not have been able to live with himself afterwards.

They ran out of the room swiftly, down the stairs and through the archway. Behind them the Shadows converged, moving together like a massive tidal wave. Sam threw some of her Magic over her shoulder, aiming at the mass as Malachi moved to the wall furthest from it, quickly drawing glowing symbols on the wall. Jamie recognised enough of them to know that he was building a portal.

Madison and Danny stood shoulder to shoulder in front of Malachi, guarding him so that he could finish building their escape route, Jade also stood behind them as she was the only one without any use of Magic to protect herself.

Sam's Magic went right through the Shadows, her Power

appearing to have no effect on the creature . . . or whatever it was.

From somewhere behind, he heard Jack cry out.

Jamie turned to him, immediately thinking that perhaps he had been attacked by whatever the enemy was, but Jack was nowhere near the Shadows.

He was in the brightest corner of the room, his back pressed against the stone wall as he clutched at his chest, his jaw clenching in pain, his eyes squeezed tightly shut. Jamie stepped towards him, but was pushed back by Sam. Her hand gripped Jack's shoulder as she gazed at him with a great amount of concern. "What's wrong?" she asked. "Did something get you?"

Jack shook his head, breathing heavily through his nose as he bit down on his lip to keep himself from crying out any more.

Behind them, Malachi shouted that the portal was done and urged everyone through it.

Jade was the first in, followed quickly by Madison.

Danny stood there for a moment. "Sam, come on!"

Sam waved him away without looking in his direction, her attention fully focused on Jack as she indicated for him to go on without her.

After a moment of hesitation, he did.

Sam grabbed Jack by the arm and pulled him roughly to his feet. Jack walked with her as best he could, shuffling along the tiles with great difficulty.

Jamie ran to the other side of him and helped Sam to carry him along.

Behind them, the Shadows drew closer.

Jack fell to his knees, crying out with pain once more. His screams echoed through the small area in which they stood and into the hall beyond. He moved both of his hands on his head, entangling his fingers in his hair. "Get out you hags!" he screamed. "Leave me alone!"

"What's wrong?" Sam shouted over the noise of the screams, though Jack didn't seem to hear her.

His hands began to shake and slowly he clenched them into fists. His body began to follow suit and it looked as though he was having a seizure. As his body writhed on the floor, his appearance began to shift, somehow making him appear more non-corporeal than usual.

"Come on!" Malachi shouted from the portal.

"Jack!" Sam knelt down beside him, her eyes wide and panicked. Though Jamie did not fully understand what was happening to Jack, he could tell from the unadulterated fear in Sam's expression that it was nothing good. "You need to be okay, we have to go."

Jack looked up at her, his shoulders shaking as he forced the words out through his pain. "Then go."

"No . . . " Sam shook her head, her jaw clenched stubbornly. "I'm not going *anywhere* without you."

"I'm already dead, Sam! Go!"

"No!"

Sam grabbed Jack by the arm and tried to drag him towards the portal.

The Shadows were now close enough that if any of them were to reach out they could have touched them. Their proximity caused a great terror in Jamie's heart, and so he grabbed Jack by the other arm and tried to help Sam pull him forward.

It was no use.

Even their combined strength couldn't move him. It was as though his body was frozen in place being held by some unseen force.

The Shadows rolled over Jack's feet. Jamie looked on in

horror as they became lost in the darkness and he seemed to become part of the mist.

As the two non-corporal entities met they seemed to mingle, the stronger and darker of the two absorbing the weaker . . . which was Jack.

Sam stayed with him still, refusing to heed Jack's urgings and get through the portal even though it was now obvious there was nothing to be done.

Jack pulled his arms away and slammed them to the floor, pushing himself up with great difficulty, his face red with the effort.

Without a moment's hesitation, he reached towards Sam and shoved her with significant strength. She fell backwards and skidded across the floor, landing by Malachi's feet.

She looked to Jack, her lips parted in shock, her eyes red and watering.

Jack grabbed hold of Jamie's wrist and pulled him close, staring him straight in the eyes as the Shadows crawled over his back and continued to deconstruct his physical form, his hands fading even as they held onto Jamie's arm. "I'm already dead," he whispered, and Jamie knew that it was true. There was nothing anyone could do to save Jack. Half of him had already been consumed by the monstrous creature that slowly crawled its way over him and towards the rest of them. "She's the important one."

There was no saving Jack.

These were the unspoken words that clung in the air between them as Jack's eyes bore into his.

A hard lump formed in Jamie's throat as he nodded his head, reluctantly accepting the silent request that Jack had placed on him. Jack's hand slipped away and he fell back to the floor no longer having the strength to keep himself upright.

In his peripheral he saw Sam scramble to her feet and run towards them once more.

Without giving Sam a chance to reach them Jamie ran at her, wrapping his arm around her waist and lifting her off her feet. Holding onto her tightly as she kicked and scratched at him in an attempt to get herself free. "Get off me!" she screamed. "What are you doing! Go back!" she cried, unwilling to accept that there was nothing to be done.

When he refused to turn back or put her down she screamed unintelligibly, clawing at his hands so hard she drew blood and kicking at his legs with such force that his knees buckled.

"Go back! Put me down! We can't leave him! Don't leave him!"

Jamie clenched his eyes shut, ignoring her pleading with great difficulty. His heart pounded in his chest and stabbed with pain as he dragged Sam away from Jack and the Shadows that tainted him.

"Please!" she cried as they neared the portal. "Jamie, *please!*" She was crying now and though he could not see her tears he could hear her sobs. "*Jamie PLEASE!* You can't leave him . . . He's all I have. He's all I have! You have you let me go back! Go back, he's all that I have!"

Jamie's eyes stung with tears as her words drove knives right though his soul, but he still did the only thing he could do, and brought Sam through the portal.

The last thing he saw as he pulled her through was the light dim from Jack's eyes just before he was completely swallowed by the darkness.

CHAPTER 60

The Shadows dispersed soon after the Witch had made her escape. They no longer seemed interested in the dealings of the seers once there was no prospect of the Witch returning and no hope of them achieving their revenge through the use of prophecies.

However, Atropos was not about to give up on herself and her sisters that easily.

They had the prophecies to hand and had worked long and hard to ensure that what was written would come to pass.

All they had to do was to now take a more active part in their assurances to leave no room for failure.

They had previously ignored the Vampire's presence around the Witch, sure that he would hold no sway in the overall outcome of events. After all, he was nothing but a mere Vampire and held no place within their prophecies, and was therefore undeserving of further attention.

However, after how this meeting had turned out, ignoring

the Vampire was not a mistake they were likely to make a second time.

With a sigh, Atropos turned to her sisters and asked, "Where is the cloth that holds the prophecy?"

Before they could answer, someone unknown to them whispered, "Which prophecy?"

Atropos turned sharply at the sound of a voice that did not belong to either of her sisters. At the bottom of the staircase stood a young girl, with white hair, white skin and red eyes. She was dressed in the garb of the modern day which was unexpected of anyone who dared to enter this temple of their own free will.

"Who—"

"Did you mean this one?" The girl pulled a cloth from behind her back and held it up for them to see. On it was written, not a prophecy, but one of the possible outcomes for the life of the Witch—the outcome that would have been most likely before the prophecy had been written.

She threw the cloth, where it landed softly on the marble steps.

Atropos looked to her sisters, both of whom were staring at the girl wide eyed and open mouthed. Their expressions told Atropos everything she needed to know, that she wasn't the only seer who could not identify the girl from anywhere in existence.

This girl was just as invisible to them.

"Or . . . maybe you meant this one? . . . Or this one?"

The girl pulled out two more cloths and held one in each hand. One was the prophecy that had been written for the Witch, the one that spoke of her stopping the war. The other cloth was new, and on it was stitched a future that Atropos had never seen before.

The girl looked to the cloth she held in her left hand. "She is the key to stopping a war that has lasted a millennia. Her soul bound to that of her ancestor. Power greater than the source of all Magic. Through loss of blood and sacrifice of life she will end the war only by honouring the blood oath of her predecessor . . . blah blah blah." The girl threw the cloth on top of the other. "I don't really like that one."

"Who —"

The girl interrupted once more. "But then, I suppose, since it's the prophecy that was never meant to be there wasn't really any possibility of me liking it, was there?" She looked to them for a moment, as if expecting them to attempt to answer her rhetorical question. She sighed when no one spoke. "I do like this one though." She held up the last cloth. "It's not really a prophecy though. See I'm not much of a puppetmaster . . . All that following people around and orchestrating events . . . It's boring and tiring and, well, I suppose I'm just not bothered enough in most cases. I am a *really* good psychic though." She took a step towards them as she spoke.

"And see, unlike you three I aim to do the job properly. I look to the future and see *all* of the possibilities and well . . . most psychics always latch on to the outcome that seems the most likely. But we all know that in Sam's case the most likely one just isn't possible any more, not with all of the messing around you three did. And to tell you the truth, I suppose I've always had a bit of a soft spot for the underdog. Especially when rooting for the least likely outcome is the *only* way to prevent a faked prophecy."

"What —"

"Oh please," the girl smiled. "Help yourself. Have a look."

She threw the cloth forward, where it landed on top of the others.

Atropos ran and picked it up, straightening it out so that

she could read. Her sisters both crowded around her, reading the possibility over her shoulder.

The girl walked over to them and smiled. "You wanna know the best part about this possibility? All they had to do was meet, and after that the rest takes care of itself."

The girl directed to the words embedded within the threads. "See all of this . . . that's just pure stubbornness so, I'm pretty sure he'll win."

Atropos threw the cloth to the floor. "This possibility is so miniscule—"

"Yes." She nodded her head. "So miniscule that you completely overlooked it, even though it says right there, 'He is the key to her downfall.' Now, if there was anything written anywhere that mentioned someone was a key to *my* downfall, it wouldn't matter how microscopic the possibility, I would pay attention."

Atropos smirked. "Well, girl, thank you for bringing this to our attention. We'll be sure to deal with this accordingly."

She raised her arm to call forth the Shadows to carry a message to Kon.

She felt the smile fall from her face when nothing happened.

The girl laughed a little. "Yeah, I'm not stupid. I cut you off when I got here . . . I'm not here to help you. You three have been very naughty and I'm here to put a stop to it."

The girl threw her arm out and released a blast of silver energy that knocked all three of them to the floor, leaving them sprawled in the centre of their alter. "Don't worry, I'm just going to cleanse you, not kill you. I'm going to need some help fixing the mess you've made."

"Who are you?" Atropos screamed as her body locked in position, preventing her from moving. "What do you want!"

"I'm Effie," the girl said with another smile, "and I want

the Vampire to win."

<u>**AND SOME FINAL WORDS . . .**</u>

As this book is self published and I lack the advertising and marketing budget of more traditionally published books, my main form of advertising comes from you guys (the readers).

So please, if you liked, loved, hated, despised or felt/thought anything about this book at all, leave me a review and let me and others know what you thought.

Visit me online for book updates and some of my insane ramblings about life and stuff:

evilbunnybooks.com